Jessica spun around to lean against the rail with all the nonchalance she could muster. "What," she asked softly, "makes you think I'm the right woman for you?"

Lucas's face hardened at the condescension in her words, but he undertook to answer the question. "Don't forget, lady, I've seen the other side of you. I've seen you looking dirty and disheveled and fighting mad. And I've known what it's like to hold you in my arms and have you give yourself completely to me."

Possession shone in his eyes.

"Oh, yes, Jessica Travers. You're the right woman for me."

STEPHANIE JAMES

is a pseudonym for bestselling, award-winning author **Jayne Ann Krentz**. Under various pseudonyms—including Jayne Castle and Amanda Quick—Ms. Krentz has over twenty-two million copies of her books in print. Her fans admire her versatility as she switches between historical, contemporary and futuristic romances. She attributes a "lifelong addiction to romantic daydreaming" as the chief influence on her writing. With her husband, Frank, she currently resides in the Pacific Northwest.

JAYNE ANN KRENTZ
WRITING AS

Stephanie James

THE SILVER SNARE

Silhouette Books

Published by Silhouette Books
America's Publisher of Contemporary Romance

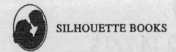 SILHOUETTE BOOKS

ISBN 0-373-80680-9

THE SILVER SNARE

Copyright © 1983 by Jayne Ann Krentz

This edition published by arrangement with Harlequin Books S.A.

® and TM are trademarks of Harlequin Books S.A., used under license.
Trademarks indicated with ® are registered in the United States Patent
and Trademark Office, the Canadian Trade Marks Office and in other
countries.

Visit us at www.romance.net

Printed in U.S.A.

For my brother Jim, who's doing better in the stock market than I am. But what the heck, I'm not the envious sort. All my love, and just see if I give you another market tip!

One

The clash of wills occurred within hours after the commuter plane shuddered to a jarring halt on the floor of the desert canyon. Jessica Travers lost the battle—decisively.

She had moved instinctively into the power vacuum that had developed among the handful of frightened passengers, operating with the calm authority of a woman who was accustomed to bringing order out of chaos. It had been her fate to have the seat closest to the small door of the de Havilland Twin Otter; she had gotten it open almost before the plane had skewed to a halt. Then she had reached for the seat belts of the two children sitting on the opposite side of the twenty-passenger craft. Thank God there are only seven people on board beside the pilot and co-pilot, she thought as she hustled the two wide-eyed children out the door and turned to give quiet, forceful orders to the pair of elderly women seated farther forward.

The women obeyed with compelling urgency, assisted by the young man ahead of them. As the three of them exited the cabin, Jessica glanced back with a frown, mentally counting heads. There should have been one more passenger, she thought, bracing herself for the leap onto the ground.

Then she saw him, the quiet man with the iron-gray eyes who had been sitting far forward. He had ducked into the cockpit and now he was hurrying back down the narrow aisle.

"Pilot's dead. Can't tell about the other one. Get the hell out!"

Jessica hitched up the skirt of the ivory gabardine suit and jumped, her high-heeled sandals clutched in one hand. The man with the iron-colored eyes was right behind her. Together they raced to join the others, who hovered at a safe distance. The entire evacuation had taken only seconds.

For a critical few moments everyone stood in shaky, stunned silence, waiting to see if the plane would explode into flames. Then, without a word, Jessica joined the quiet man when he started purposefully back toward the stricken aircraft.

"Stay here," he ordered, as he realized she was accompanying him.

Jessica ignored him. "If the co-pilot's injured you'll need help getting him out. It doesn't look as if the plane's going to catch fire."

The co-pilot was unconscious. Together they pulled him from the cockpit and settled him gently on the ground. The waning desert sun beat down on the small group as they gathered around anxiously. Jessica knelt beside the injured man and examined him, using the basic first aid techniques she had learned in a course given to her staff of hotel employees two years earlier. Her gently probing fingers found the swelling bulge on the back of his head.

"We'll have to assume concussion at this point," she sighed, getting to her feet. "Let's see if we can get him into the shade."

It was obvious the rest of the group was accepting her leadership and that of the man beside her. Jessica took the implied responsibility with an equanimity born of experience. She was accustomed to being the one in charge.

"I'm Lucas Kincaid," the gray-eyed man told her as they worked together that afternoon supervising the unloading of the aircraft and soothing the anxieties of the others.

"Jessica Travers. Call me Jessie," she offered in return.

For a time they had worked in harmony, each assuming different chores. It was Lucas who, with the aid of the young man named Dave, took charge of burying the pilot. Jessica assigned the two elderly sisters to soothe the children's fears and then climbed back into the plane to see how many sandwiches had been packed on board as snacks for the passengers. They were in luck. Most commuter planes this size carried no food at all, but the airline had been competing for customers, apparently, and had started offering some light fare. The co-pilot was to have passed out the plastic-wrapped sandwiches at midpoint in the flight, together with a canned drink.

Water, fortunately, was not going to be a problem. The stream running through the desert canyon flowed clear and clean.

Sensing the innate authority in the two strong-minded people who had taken charge, the other passengers seemed more than willing to do as they were told. The trouble didn't start until the instructions Jessica and Lucas were giving began to conflict.

Confusion was the first response when Lucas calmly countermanded an order Jessica had given for the collection of firewood. Several other incidents followed until a new and more immediate tension began to ripple through the small group. Jessica felt it almost at once. She had enough experience handling people to know what was happening. The group would follow the strongest leader. It was as if they were a herd of wild animals waiting for the order of dominance to be clearly established.

The clash of wills grew steadily more imminent during the afternoon. Even the children were looking confused and anxious, their eyes moving questioningly from one adult to the other. It was clear a battle was shaping up over the issue of who would be in charge.

Jessica, accustomed to the refinements of an established corporate structure, which frowned on open warfare in favor of subtle behind-the-scenes maneuvering, was unprepared for the manner of confrontation Lucas forced upon her, however. Instead of a quiet argument carried out away from the others, he brought matters to a head in front of the rest of the passengers.

She knew instinctively that he'd done it that way on purpose. The man wanted no question as to which of them had won the battle. His primitive approach to leadership angered her.

In the end Lucas chose a relatively minor issue, an excuse really, to bring the conflict out into the open. Later Jessica remembered only that the war had been conducted over an insignificant discussion about what to use for boiling stream water.

"That's enough, Jessie," Lucas had announced in his soft, gravelly voice as he rose slowly to his feet beside the fire he'd been building. "I think it's time we solved the problem which seems to be developing here."

There was enough steel buried in his words to catch the attention of the others at once. A taut, curious silence descended on the small group. Everyone, including Jessica, knew the showdown had arrived.

Slowly she eyed the man who was challenging the authority she wielded so automatically. As if in response to an invitation for physical battle, her senses leaped into full alert, the adrenaline pouring into her bloodstream.

Lucas Kincaid was not particularly tall, probably about five-foot ten or eleven inches, but there was a compact, lean strength in him that registered itself at once. The faded jeans he was wearing rode low on narrow hips, fitting closely to the smoothly muscled thighs. The khaki shirt stretched across sinewy shoulders and the hard planes of his chest. The clothing didn't reveal an ounce of fat and Jessica doubted there was any to be found on that strong, well-coordinated frame.

The quiet power in his body was mirrored in the bluntly carved lines of a fiercely unhandsome face and in the cool, watchful depths of iron-gray eyes. Lucas Kincaid was probably around thirty-five or thirty-six, Jessica estimated; he exuded masculine authority. He exerted it now with the confident dominance of a man who was accustomed to command. Military? she wondered fleetingly. Perhaps someone who had once captained a ship? Certainly he wasn't from her own polished world of sophisticated hotels and beautifully organized conventions.

She knew what he saw when he looked at her, and the knowledge didn't add to her composure. The ivory business suit was dusty and stained, although the narrow skirt and the tiny-collared yellow blouse revealed the full curve of her hips, her small waist, and the gentle shape of her small, tip-tilted breasts. Her tawny brown hair was straggling free from the sleek twist at the back of her head, and curling tendrils fell down around her shoulders.

No, she wasn't looking her executive suite best, but the disarray in her appearance did nothing to hide the clear intelligence in her aquamarine eyes or the feminine strength in a face which, while certainly not beautiful, was capable of drawing the attention of the discerning. There was a striking energy and competence in the firm lines of her nose and chin and, underlying those qualities, a gentleness that she rarely allowed to surface. Gentleness and softness were not qualities that would have stood her in good stead in her world, so Jessica had learned early to restrain them. She was twenty-nine years old, but she had been accustomed to positions of responsibility since she had been graduated from college and had gone into hotel management.

Jessica faced her opponent, for that was how she now thought of Lucas, with a steady authority that spoke volumes and rendered her tousled appearance unimportant.

"We're all in this together," she declared forcefully. "Therefore the decisions that affect our future should be mutually agreed upon."

"This is not the sort of situation where consensus will work," Lucas told her flatly, his hands planted implacably on his lean hips as he regarded her with narrowed eyes. "Not even a consensus of two. Since I am not prepared to put my life in your hands and let you make the decisions which will be called for until we're rescued, we're left with only one viable option."

"I'm to put my life in *your* hands, is that it? Let you make the decisions which will decide our fate?" she demanded scornfully. Why did he have to handle it this way in front of the others? Why couldn't he have been a gentleman about the situation? There were more subtle ways of conducting such infighting.

"Yes." His answer was totally unyielding.

"Why should I do that? I see no reason why matters can't be evaluated and discussed as they arise." She felt the tension mount as she tossed the challenge back at him. This man wasn't going to back down. She

knew it with sudden certainty. And if he wasn't going
to retreat, that left her with little alternative. To drag
out the war would be stupid and harmful to the others.
Common sense told her as much, even as her pride
urged rebellion.

"We're not going to conduct town-hall meetings on
every issue which comes up. We don't have that luxury. Take my word for it, if you don't already know
it; things can fall apart very quickly in a situation like
this. More important, *people* can fall apart. We have
no way of knowing how long we're going to be stuck
here and that fact alone will contribute to a breakdown
in morale. Discipline and a clearly established line of
authority are our best defense. When you get back to
civilization you can sue me for assuming command
without benefit of a vote! But from now until help
arrives, this is the way it's going to be. I'm in charge.
You will take orders from me and you will not counter
any of my instructions."

"Give me one good reason for appointing you our
unquestioned leader!"

"I know how to survive out here. I know what we
can eat and what will poison us. I know how to shelter
us from the sun during the day and how to keep us
warm at night. I know how to use the materials from
the plane to best advantage and," he paused in the
rapid-fire list so that the next words would have
greater impact, "I am tougher and stronger than you
are, Jessie Travers. If you want a knock-down drag-
out battle to prove it, I'm willing to demonstrate."

Jessica caught her breath in amazement, a flush of
anger surging into her cheeks as she realized he meant

it. Lucas Kincaid was assuming control and he was prepared to enforce his rule with violence.

The resentment in her soared, but there was another element with which to contend. She was intelligent enough to believe him when he said he knew what he was doing out here in the middle of the California desert mountains. It was Lucas who had determined earlier that there was no hope of getting the plane back off the ground. Too much damage had been done during the emergency landing. And it was Lucas who had revealed the treasures in his fishing tackle box, which he had unloaded from the baggage compartment. Jessica knew the knife and other assorted implements might make all the difference in how well they ate during the next few days. And it was Lucas who knew how to use those essential tools. He knew what he was doing and he had the innate air of command that would make the others follow his orders. She might not like the way he was handling matters, but if this was the only way in which he would give the group the benefit of his knowledge, there wasn't much choice for her. She acknowledged to herself that on some very basic level she trusted him. Jessica didn't particularly like the man, but she *trusted* him.

"I'm not going to fight you for the role of exalted leader, Lucas," she told him coolly. She could almost hear the relief that went through the other passengers.

"You're accepting my authority?" he pressed.

Jessica arched one eyebrow. "You can do as you like. I wouldn't dream of engaging in a wrestling match with the one person in the crowd who owns a knife. As you suggested, I'll wait until we're rescued before I sue!''

He ignored her attempt at flippancy. ''That's not good enough. Not nearly good enough, Jessie,'' Lucas told her very quietly. The iron in his eyes sent a shiver along her nerve endings.

''What do you want from me?'' she blazed, embarrassed and infuriated over the fact that he was dragging out the scene, now that he had what he sought.

''I want absolute and unquestioning acceptance of my authority. I want to know you'll obey me without any argument or prolonged discussion. I want to know that if I tell you to jump you'll jump. Without complaining! Do I make myself very clear?''

''Very,'' she breathed angrily. ''But I fail to see why you have to take such a feudal approach!''

''Because if I don't, you'll cause trouble from day one,'' he growled. ''You have enough power to split the group into two factions and I think you know it. You can sow dissension and discontent. That sort of thing could cost us our lives if we're here very long. I'm taking steps to ensure our survival by ensuring your obedience.''

He was right, Jessica admitted silently, as they faced each other. His way might anger her, but it might also stand the best chance of working. Lucas Kincaid's survival skills might be all that stood between them and disaster. Out of the corner of her eye she saw the frightened, anxious expressions on the children's faces. The elderly women waited tight-lipped for the results of the showdown and the young man focused his whole attention on Lucas, which didn't particularly surprise Jessica. Dave was sporting a military-style haircut and appeared to be only recently out of boot camp. He was responding readily to the dominance in the older man.

"There's no need to play feudal lord," Jessica began determinedly, but even she could hear the surrender in her voice.

"There's every need," Lucas countered roughly. "Everyone in the group has to know exactly where you stand. I want to hear you say you'll follow orders and give me your full support."

She could feel the waves of his willpower lapping at her, reaching out to drag her under. There was no real choice, not in this time and in this place. The stakes were too basic, too critical. Lucas Kincaid wanted complete power and in exchange he offered the best hope of survival.

With a small exclamation of disgust aimed mostly at herself for the act of surrender, she nodded her head once in submission.

"All right, Lucas. You're in charge. I will do as you say."

"No arguments?"

"When you get back home, I suggest you sign up for some of the new management training techniques," she said dryly. "Your approach is a little unpolished."

"Answer me!" he grated.

Jessica blinked. "No arguments," she agreed softly. Inwardly she was seething.

He studied her coldly for a moment longer, as if assessing the depths of her submission; then apparently satisfied, he turned away on one booted heel to issue a series of instructions that sent the others scurrying in several directions. When he'd finished, he turned back to Jessica. "You can get those sandwiches ready. We'll have them for dinner. Not much large enough to eat in that stream."

Jessica resisted the urge to say "Yes, Sir!" Without a word she started toward the box of food. She felt the iron eyes following her for a moment longer, but she didn't glance back.

Later as they sat around the fire on the seat cushions they had removed from the plane's cabin, Lucas explained that they would stay with the plane.

"Our best bet is the ELT," he said quietly in response to a query from Dave.

"What's an ELT?" Abby, one of the two older women, asked. Sharon and Matt, the children, listened solemnly.

"It stands for *Emergency Locating Transmitter*. All aircraft are required to carry them now. I checked earlier and it's functioning, putting out a signal which can be detected for about a hundred and fifty miles. That's the way the searchers will home in on us."

Before she could stop herself, Jessica asked the first question which popped into her head. "But won't the walls of the canyons block that signal?"

"To some extent, yes. It may take a while for people to find us, but they *will* find us. All we have to do is stay alive and healthy until someone picks up that signal."

The others nodded, accepting his certainty of rescue with gratitude. Jessica frowned thoughtfully, glancing across at the co-pilot who had been swimming in and out of consciousness all afternoon. "What killed the pilot? The rest of us survived the landing."

"My guess is he was dead before we hit the ground," Lucas said. "He didn't appear to be injured. A heart attack, perhaps. We probably owe our lives to the co-pilot, who had to take over at the last minute."

Jessica said nothing further. She was keeping her communications with Lucas short and to the point. The memory of the humiliating scene he had put her through earlier would stay with her a long, long time, regardless of how soon help arrived. She felt his eyes on her from time to time during the evening, but she was careful to give him no opportunity to complain about her behavior. Her submission had at least one good side benefit, she noted wryly. The rest of the small group had relaxed and were now functioning as a team, their confidence in Lucas plain to see.

She awoke often during that first night, shifting uncomfortably on the bed of seat cushions and adjusting the makeshift covers. From time to time she crawled stiffly out of bed to check on the condition of the co-pilot, whose name, according to the small tag on his uniform, was Gary Franklin. She had changed earlier into a pair of fashionable mocha suede pants. She'd packed them for the resort to which she had been heading when the plane went down; she was glad now of the added warmth. They weren't in any danger of freezing here in the canyon, but the night was chill, nevertheless.

The fire was burning low, but it gave off a certain primitive comfort just by its presence. Jessica knelt beside Gary and automatically checked his pulse. He didn't seem to be getting any worse, she thought in relief. Placing her hand on his brow, she noted a faint warmth, though, and hoped he wasn't in danger of developing a fever.

About to crawl back to her crude bed, Jessica realized that the little girl, Sharon, was watching her, a silent plea in her blue eyes as she lay very still beneath the sheepskin jacket Lucas had provided as a blanket.

Responding to that ancient call for comfort, Jessica moved over to the child.

"Warm enough, honey?" she whispered, adjusting the jacket with a soothing touch.

Mutely, the little girl nodded. Then a tiny tear trickled down her cheek, reflecting in the firelight. "Do you think my daddy will be looking for Matt and me? We were on our way to visit him."

"Oh, yes; by now he'll be looking very hard for you and Matt," Jessica murmured, her heart going out to the frightened child. "He'll have a lot of people helping him look, too, you know. They'll find us, don't worry. And until they do find us, Lucas will take care of everything." She amazed herself with the ready way the assurance came to her lips. Strange how you could trust a man you never wanted to see again!

"Lucas was mad at you this afternoon, wasn't he?" Sharon whispered anxiously.

With a stifled sigh, Jessica responded to the need for reassurance. "Yes, he was," she said calmly. "I was arguing with him, you see. I won't argue with him anymore."

"My mommy and daddy used to argue a lot. Then

Daddy went away. Now Matt and I only get to visit him when school is over for the year.''

The unspoken question behind the words came through to Jessica and her mouth curved ruefully. "You don't have to worry, honey. I won't argue with Lucas and he won't go away and leave us."

"Good." Sharon yawned and settled down into the cushions. "Matt hates arguments," she explained with the maturity of an older sister.

"I know how he feels," Jessica grumbled under her breath as she gave in to the impulse to bend down and kiss the girl's forehead.

Then she climbed to her feet and moved silently back toward her own pile of cushions, the socks Dave had loaned her giving little protection against the hard ground. It was going to be a long night.

She was halfway back around the fire, moving past Lucas's quiet form, when he snaked out a strong hand and encircled her ankle. Startled, Jessica swallowed an exclamation of surprise and glanced down. In the dancing firelight she saw the intent gray eyes studying her. She came to a halt and waited obediently.

"Thanks for the vote of confidence," he muttered in that dark, gravelly voice.

"Hardly necessary," she drawled softly. "You're not running this show by putting matters to a vote." The fingers around her ankle tightened dangerously.

"No arguments, remember? You promised me and you just promised Sharon."

Jessica closed her eyes for a few seconds, drawing strength and patience.

"No arguments. You're welcome to the vote of confidence." She opened her eyes again and waited for him to release her.

"Thanks. When this is all over are you ever going to speak to me again?" he demanded, almost whimsically, examining her shadowed features.

"When this is all over," Jessica responded carefully, "I doubt that we shall ever see each other again. The issue won't arise."

He let that pass. "About what happened this afternoon..."

Jessica waited. Was he going to apologize?

"I had to do it, you know. You're a strong-willed woman. You could have been very dangerous."

"Don't worry, I'm not going to play Mr. Christian to your Captain Bligh." No, there wouldn't be any apology from this man. An explanation perhaps, from time to time, but never an apology.

"Good. I'd hate to have to order you to be tied to the mast and flogged!" he said wryly, releasing her ankle as if her skin had become overly warm to the touch. He turned his back on her, apparently going back to sleep without any effort at all. Cautiously, feeling as if she'd had a near miss, Jessica made her way back to her bedding. She fell asleep with the memory of strong fingers wrapped around her ankle, chaining her.

During the next three days, Lucas saw to it that their lives were orderly and disciplined. Everyone had jobs, even the children, and the work was excellent therapy, Jessica acknowledged privately. Each person felt as if he or she were making a contribution to the group's survival, although there was never any question but that each looked to Lucas for leadership and direction. The co-pilot seemed to be recovering, although Jessica kept him quiet and firmly ensconced on his pile of cushions. He occasionally complained of double vision and headaches, but there seemed to be no fever or other problem. He was content to rest. He agreed with Lucas's guess about the pilot.

"Right after we got into trouble, he told me he might not make it. He was in a lot of pain during the last few minutes. I'm sure it was his heart," Gary said quietly at one point as he sipped the tea they had made from some leaves off a scrubby bush Lucas had identified and pronounced safe. "I did a hell of a job on that landing, didn't I?" he added with a regretful sigh as he morosely viewed the crippled de Havilland.

"Yes," Lucas told him firmly, "you did. We all walked away from it, didn't we?" He slapped the younger man on the shoulder and got to his feet.

"Lucky he was along on the flight, wasn't it?" Gary asked thoughtfully as he finished his tea and watched Lucas moving off toward the stream.

Jessica, who was waiting to take the soft drink can she had given him to use as a cup, nodded once, saying nothing.

The sandwiches ran out the second day and when Lucas disappeared with Dave for an entire afternoon and returned to camp with a brace of dead rabbits, there was mixed reaction. The children were horrified. Abby and her sister Mabel nodded appreciatively. Gary viewed the returning hunters hungrily. Jessica went forward to take the small, furry bodies with practical nonchalance.

"Here, give me those. You guys look exhausted."

"You know what to do with them?" Lucas asked in surprise, releasing the trophies.

"You're looking at someone who routinely plans food for five hundred people or more," she told him wryly. "I've done my stint in the Scanlon kitchens. Management likes its executives to get *involved* in the basic elements of the hotel business."

"Scanlon?" he questioned curiously. "The Scanlon hotel chain?"

She nodded. "I'll take them down to the stream and clean them." She lifted one brow with silent taunting. "Women's work, I'd say, wouldn't you?"

He let that one go, probably because he didn't want to have to clean the rabbits himself, Jessica concluded.

It wasn't until the meat was broiling over the fire that Sharon and Matt finally made known their feelings on the matter of eating rabbits.

"Yuck." That was from Matt, who nevertheless sniffed the smell of the sizzling meat with an attitude of expectancy.

"You're not supposed to eat rabbits," Sharon remarked reproachfully.

"One eats what is available," Abby Morgan told the child calmly. "I've eaten many a rabbit in my day." It was she who was in charge of roasting the creatures.

The two children turned faintly accusing eyes on Lucas, who surprised Jessica by throwing up his hands in mock defense. "Don't look at me like that," he begged solemnly. "This is as hard on me as it is on you. Back in San Diego I run a pet shop. How do you think I'm going to go home and look the bunnies in the face again?''

For an instant Jessica stared at him and then, unable to resist the impulse, she broke into unexpected, outright laughter. "A pet shop! I don't believe it!"

He glanced up, catching her eye over the top of Sharon's mop of blond hair. "It's true. What did you think I do for a living?" But there was a new element in the iron-gray eyes, something approaching laughter, perhaps, and something more, something infinitely dangerous to a woman.

"I hadn't given it much thought," she said quickly, turning back to the wild roots she was cooking on a sheet of metal retrieved from the plane. It was Lucas, of course, who had dug up the roots and pronounced them edible. "But I certainly wouldn't have guessed that you run a pet shop!"

"But, then, you don't know much about me, do you?" he pointed out quietly.

A faint tremor went through Jessica and she concentrated very hard on the cooking roots. "No." And I don't want to know very much, she added silently to herself. It's better if I don't. Safer.

She couldn't have explained how she had reached that conclusion, but a part of her was firmly convinced it was nothing less than the truth. It was important that she didn't relax around Lucas Kincaid. There was a tension between the two of them which, while it grew out of their initial conflict, seemed to encompass far more than a mere clash between two strong-willed people. She had known that when she'd found herself watching him in idle moments, found herself aware of him as more than a fellow survivor of a disaster. God help her, she was seeing him as a man, a male animal, and that was frightening. What made it worse and far more dangerous, was that some instinct told her he had begun to see her as more than a woman for whom he had assumed temporary responsibility. Was he seeing her as a woman who now belonged to him?

Whatever was happening between them must be firmly squelched, Jessica knew. Her mind resisted the words, for it was as if naming the tension would make it more lethal; more real. But her body recognized it with an unerring instinct that was older than time. No, she must walk carefully around this threatening element that had crept into the atmosphere between them. Lucas Kincaid had assumed absolute control over the group, but his power didn't extend to claiming her for his bed.

On the afternoon of the third day, the females in the crowd opted for a bath in the upper reaches of the cold stream. The men were banished and Sharon, Abby, Mabel, and Jessica frolicked, naked, in the chill waters, reveling in the opportunity to wash their hair and feel clean once more. There was a great deal of giggling and splashing before they emerged one by one to dry themselves on the cotton flower-print dress Mabel had designated as a towel.

"I never did like this dress," she admitted engagingly, as she used it to vigorously rub a laughing Sharon.

Dressed once again, they were striding, single-file, back toward camp, where the men waited to take their places in the stream, when the faintest movement at the edge of her vision caused Jessica to glance curiously up at the rugged canyon wall.

For an instant she could see nothing against the bright glare of desert sunlight. Then her breath caught in her throat as she halted, unnoticed, at the rear of the line. Lucas was up there, lounging with deceptive casualness on a sun-warmed rock. There was another dead rabbit dangling from the belt at his waist.

His eyes met hers as she stood staring up at him. He had been watching, Jessica realized, stricken. He had watched her bathing among the others and she knew now beyond a shadow of a doubt that he wanted her.

The knowledge surged through her senses, devastating them. For an eternity she stood in the sand beside the stream feeling singled out, earmarked, and trapped by the dominant male in the herd. Her wet hair gleamed in the sunlight, dampening the poppy-colored blouse she was wearing. A feeling of panic gripped her as she read the implacable expression carved in harsh lines on his tanned face.

The panic, she realized, horrified, wasn't so much over her patent helplessness if he chose to pursue her; rather, it was being generated by the reaction she was experiencing. There was a sense of primitive rightness about the silent claim his eyes told her he was staking. Her body was choosing to recognize that claim and accept it.

Shocked, Jessica tore her gaze away from the silent hunter on the rock. Hurrying, she trotted after the other women, instinctively seeking safety in a crowd. My God, she thought frantically, what's happening to me?

I'm not a...a female animal to be claimed by the strongest male in the group! I don't even like the man!

Nothing was said as the afternoon turned into evening. Once again there was rabbit for supper and this time the children didn't complain. Jessica, who had been avoiding Lucas's eyes since he had returned to camp, sat tensely on her pile of cushions, eating the meat he had trapped in a snare made of fishing line.

She was chewing the sizzling, juicy food with actual enjoyment, when the inevitable occurred. Her aquamarine gaze accidentally collided with the waiting iron trap of his eyes across the flickering flames of the fire.

Jessica froze at the message she read in those cool gray depths. She could feel him willing her to acknowledge that somehow, by some primitive right, she belonged to him. He had assumed the responsibility for protecting her. He had hunted and killed to put food in her mouth. He had forced her to accept his authority. Now he was staking the most fundamental of claims.

How long before he came to her bed?

Two

The inevitable occurred on the fourth night of the ordeal and none of Jessica's lectures to herself, none of her mental preparation, quite readied her to handle the situation when the moment arrived.

It had been a difficult day. The novelty of the experience, as well as the fear, had worn off for the children. They were feeling restless and it required considerable effort on the part of everyone to keep them occupied and out of trouble. Abby was worried about a flareup of her sister's arthritis. Dave seemed unusually morose until Lucas dispatched him to check the rabbit snares, and Gary, the co-pilot, worried Jessica by sleeping more than he had the previous day.

But Lucas held his small clan together with firmness, reassurance, and an underlying element of discipline. By dinner he had managed to exhaust everyone with a variety of chores. Each member of the group, including Jessica, was more than ready for bed.

She crawled onto the arrangement of seat cushions, fleeting thoughts of the warmth and comfort of her own bed at home going through her head. After this she would no longer complain about the problems of living in a hotel apartment provided by management!

Lucas had disappeared a few minutes earlier on a nightly walk in the moonlight, which was becoming routine for him. Jessica was deeply aware of his absence and knew she would not fall asleep until he had slipped silently back into camp and taken his own bed. Last night she had lain awake nearly an hour waiting for him to return.

She understood his need for the time to himself after the others were asleep. Lucas gave a considerable amount to the group during the day. The responsibility he had assumed was enormous and he discharged it faithfully. Jessica could well comprehend his desire for some solitude to recharge his energies. The loneliness of command, she thought to herself with a wry smile.

Again, he didn't return for almost an hour and when Jessica finally sensed his presence at the edge of the firelight, she knew that something was different tonight. This time he would not go quietly to his bed on the other side of the fire. Jessica's pulse began to beat more quickly at the telltale points of throat and wrist. Her body was reacting to the dangerous element in the atmosphere before her mind had fully understood it.

She lay with the stillness of a small animal in hiding, watching Lucas through her lashes. He stood silently in the shadows, gazing steadily at the outline of her body. She didn't dare move as a wave of electrical tension flickered between them. The others around the campfire slept peacefully, unaware of the elemental drama being played out in the moonlight.

Then he started toward her, his booted feet making barely a sound on the desert sand. Eyes half-closed and veiled with tawny lashes, Jessica watched him approach, knowing what was on his mind. Her body sang its knowledge of what he wanted.

It was up to her, she told herself. If she called out, made a small scene and awoke the others, Lucas would stop. God help her, what was she going to do? Why wasn't she arousing Abby or Mabel? Perhaps if she pretended to be asleep he would turn back to his own bed.

Before she could sort out a logical course of action, Lucas was beside her, crouching down on one knee and reaching out to finger a curling tendril of her hair as it lay across the cushion. Wordlessly she stared up at him, all pretence of sleep gone. Her nerves were thrillingly alert and wary and alive. It would have been totally impossible to fake sleep.

He knelt with his back to the firelight and his rugged face was in deep shadow even as the dying flames flared revealingly across her own taut features.

Slowly he dropped the coil of hair and moved his rough fingertips gently to the line of her cheek. Lucas traced the contours of her face deliberately, as if he would later be modeling them in clay. Jessica trembled as he stroked her jaw to her chin and then shaped the outline of her lips. She realized with exquisite sensitivity that she wasn't the only one trembling. The force of his desire communicated itself on a fundamental level, calling to her senses. He wanted her. More than that, Lucas wanted her to reciprocate the emotion.

The swelling, flashing response in her veins sent another shudder along her nerves and Jessica was appalled at the strength of her reaction. Here in the shadows, warmed by the fading fire and the power of his need, she *did* want him. Her body ached to meet the sensual demand in the man kneeling beside her, longed to please and satisfy her mate.

Unthinkingly she turned her lips into his palm as he cupped her face and dropped the gentlest of small kisses against his skin.

"Jessie!"

Her name was a tight, near-silent plea and command as his hand slid down to find her wrist. The gray depths of his eyes reflected the silver of moonlight as he slowly straightened, tugging her up beside him. Helpless in the grip of the twin trap of her own strange longing and his undeniable desire, Jessica rose obediently beside him, her eyes never leaving his face.

Without a word he reached down to snag the light-weight windbreaker she had spread over her clothed figure as a blanket; then he was moving off with her in tow, leading her away from the safety and comfort of the campfire. Jessica wasn't sure that anything could have broken the grip of those strong fingers around her wrist at that moment. Nor was she certain she would have welcomed any attempt to do so.

What was happening seemed right and inevitable. She found herself trailing Lucas in silent acquiescence as he led her along the stream to a sandy clearing swathed in privacy and moonlight. There, far out of sight and sound of the others, he halted and turned to her.

She looked up at him, her wrist still chained in his grasp, her mouth slightly parted in unconscious invitation. Her sea-colored eyes were heavy-lidded with sensual need. The longing in her sent repeated shivers through her body.

"Jessie! Jessie, I need you tonight. I want you so badly," he rasped, his voice thick and husky. His iron-gray gaze pored over her face and the fingers of his free hand came up to probe the corner of her mouth.

"I know," she managed in a bare whisper. "I know." Jessica could not have said exactly what she was acknowledging, whether it was his desire or her own. But he read the acceptance in her eyes and with a muffled groan Lucas found her mouth with his own.

The force of his kiss seemed to strangle the breath in her body. Jessica put up her hands instinctively, trying to steady herself against his shoulders as her legs weakened dangerously. The invasion of her mouth was unlike anything she had ever experienced, wiping out the memory of other men's kisses as if they had never taken place.

Lucas wrapped his arms around her fiercely, molding her to his strong, lean length with an urgency that would not now be denied. His lips moved across hers, shaping them, dampening them so that the electrical contact seemed to flow more freely from one to the other. And when she moaned softly in reaction, he seized the moment to deepen the kiss, letting his tongue surge aggressively into the dark warmth behind her lips.

Jessica's nails sank into the fabric of the khaki shirt he wore. Only that morning she had washed that shirt along with others at the stream and left it to dry on a sun-heated rock. She had chided herself for letting him force her so easily into the stereotyped female role. Now she felt as if, having washed his clothes and cooked the food he had hunted, she had some sort of claim on him—a claim equal to the one he was exerting over her.

The deeply masculine scent of him filled her nostrils as Lucas searched the interior of her mouth, conquering and coaxing and claiming. Slowly he dropped to his knees in the sand, pulling her with him. Forcing her head gently back beneath the onslaught of his kiss, he let his fingers seek out the vulnerable line of her throat.

"Lucas! Oh, Lucas..."

The sound of his name on her lips seemed to heighten the urgency in him. He tore his mouth reluctantly from hers and buried it against her throat as he found the first button of her shirt. His hand trembled slightly as he fumbled with the fastening and his lack of finesse somehow touched the womanly gentleness Jessica had learned to conceal. She sighed and leaned into him, absorbing the warmth of his body and giving him her own in return.

Slowly, a little clumsily, he undressed her, pushing aside the material of her shirt and finding the small curves of her breasts with a muted exclamation of need.

"When I saw you bathing yesterday it was all I could do not to come down and snatch you away from the others and carry you off," he breathed shakily as he discovered the hardening bud of her nipple with his thumb. "I saw the water glistening on your thighs and the way the sunlight colored your hair and I told myself you must have been meant for me. Tonight I tried to walk you out of my mind and I couldn't. I just couldn't wait any longer, Jessie."

She touched her lips to the tanned column of his neck and then nibbled experimentally at the sensitive earlobe. "I know," she said again. "When I saw you watching me I knew what was going to happen."

"God, Jessie!"

He slipped her shirt off entirely and then he began to awkwardly undo the zipper of the suede pants in which she had been sleeping. Her own fingers moving with even less assurance than his, Jessica undid the buttons of the khaki shirt, sliding her fingertips inside to find the hard planes of his chest.

She sighed as she encountered the curling crispness of hair, tracing its outline down to the flat hardness of his taut stomach. He whispered her name again and again as he shaped the outline of her hips with his palms and slid the suede pants down to her knees. Then he wrenched himself away to spread their clothing out in a semblance of a bed and settled her down onto it.

Slowly, kneeling beside her, he removed the last of her garments, exposing her slender body to the light of the desert moon. She watched him through heavy lashes as he ran his hands lightly, possessively from

her throat, down across her taut breasts, to the curve
of her thigh. The thrill her senses experienced at his
touch confused and shocked her. Her reaction to this
man was uncanny and a little stunning.

Lucas stood up then and impatiently unbuckled the
carved leather belt at his waist. He shoved aside his
own clothes until he towered over her, naked and
strong in the silvery light. Wonderingly, Jessica let her
eyes follow the sinewy line of shoulder and chest and
then sink lower to the uncompromising male hardness
of his thighs. Her nails curved into the vulnerable inner part of her palm as she absorbed the impact of him
there in the moonlight.

He came down beside her, his eyes never leaving
her face. She was gathered close against his power and
she hid her too-expressive features against his shoulder, arching luxuriously as he stroked the line of her
spine down to its base.

He caressed her body with increasing aggression,
drawing tantalizing circles on her hips one moment
and clenching his fingers tightly into her curving buttocks the next. Under his touch, Jessica began to
writhe and twist, seeking to get closer and closer so
that she could lose herself in him.

One heavy thigh trapped her languidly shifting legs,
holding her still for a moment as Lucas moved his
scorching touch along the division of her rounded bottom to the flowing warmth between her thighs.

Jessica gasped at the intimate caress, but before she
could respond he was pushing her onto her back, his
lips going to the hard peaks of her tip-tilted breasts.

"You're perfect for me," he muttered. His tongue

curled around each nipple, urging it into an even tighter bud. Then his teeth nipped excitingly until Jessica was a shivering, moaning bundle of aroused femininity beneath him.

"Lucas!"

The chill of the night was an incredible contrast to the heat of his body, she thought vaguely. It was as if all her nerves, all her senses were being brought into play for this sensual act. She was thrillingly aware of everything about the man above her, from the teasing rasp of his chest hair against her swollen breasts to the strength in the leg thrown across her thighs.

Her hands fluttered across his shoulders, her torn nails digging into the contours here and there before flitting off to explore another zone. When she found the small of his back, he pulled away slightly.

"Touch me," he half-ordered, half-pleaded and caught hold of her hand. With an aching groan he lowered it to his thigh, releasing it only when she obediently began to trace erotic little patterns there.

As if mesmerized by the wonder of him, Jessica's fingers moved closer and closer to the satin-tipped hardness of his manhood until, as if he could no longer wait for her exploring touch to find him, Lucas arched his hips, thrusting himself against her soft palm.

She gasped as he slipped into her hand, startled by the force and strength in him even as she delighted in it. For a long moment he held her close, reveling in her tender caresses, and then he freed himself to begin raining fierce kisses across her breasts and down to the curve of her stomach. Slowly he slid down her body between her legs, his fingers thrusting deeply into the silky flesh of her thighs as his kisses became more and more intimate.

When he nibbled passionately at the inside of her leg, Jessica thought she would go wild with need of him. Her fists locked violently in the pelt of his hair and she lifted her hips off the hard bed in silent confirmation of her arousal.

"Please, Lucas. Please. Now!"

Never had she felt such a stirring of violent emotion. Never had she known a man who could excite her body to such an astounding degree. Never had she known the primitive level of desire she was discovering tonight. Jessica was beyond questioning her own need. She only knew that here in the desert moonlight she must give herself to this man who was claiming her. She was his and he had every right to his claim. By the same token he belonged to her. The passion of her own claim on him was as mind-shaking as his on her. She could not, in that electric moment, conceive of ever wanting any other man but this one.

His teeth teased the silk of her inner thigh once more and then, with a low muttered cry of desire, Lucas moved back up her body, letting his fingers probe the tangle of tawny hair which shadowed the heart of her desire. She called his name with aching softness as he dazzled the most intimate secrets of her with his hand, while he kissed the curve of her shoulder hungrily.

"My woman," he breathed.

Jessica wrapped her arms around his neck. "Yes. Yes, Lucas!"

He shifted his weight, coming tightly against her

softness as he covered her length with his own. Jessica gasped as she felt him slowly, inevitably fill her completely. The thrusting impact of him made her mind swirl in a sensual vertigo. Her body accepted the invasion eagerly.

He locked them together and held them both unbearably still for a long moment as if savoring the experience to the utmost. And then, as if he could no longer restrain himself, Lucas moved against her, establishing a primeval rhythm that captured her body and chained it to his own.

Jessica gave herself up to the thrilling pattern of his lovemaking, her body responding joyously on all levels. She wrapped him close, letting him make them as one being. The coiling tension in her loins made it difficult to breathe as it tightened unbelievably. Her eyes squeezed tightly shut; her world revolved completely now around the man above her. Past and future were unimportant. Only this shivering, explosive need to satisfy and be satisfied counted in this tiny, enthralling universe.

He was losing himself in her. Jessica knew it and gloried in the knowledge. She wanted Lucas as tightly bound to her as she was to him. Together they obeyed the quickening beat of their passion until the ultimate conclusion came flashing toward them, engulfing both before they knew exactly what was happening. It was a sweeping, shattering sensation that seemed to explode the universe around them into bursting fragments of light and power.

Through the shimmering, convulsive finale, Lucas held her as if he would never let her go, her name a

muffled cry on his lips that was both an endearment
and an exclamation of masculine triumph and satisfaction.

Down, down they floated, their bodies still tightly
locked together as the aftermath of their passion made
it impossible to move for timeless moments. Slowly,
eventually, reality returned there on the floor of the
desert canyon. The soft gurgle of the stream, the quiet
sounds of the night, the even breathing of the man in
whose arms she lay, all impinged on Jessica's sense
of awareness. Tentatively, she shifted beneath the
heavy weight of him, her eyes opening languidly.

As if her small stirring were the catalyst needed to
pull him back to reality, too, Lucas raised his head
from her breast to gaze down at her softened, vulnerable face. The silver moonlight glanced off the roughly
hewn planes of his cheek and jaw and his iron-gray
eyes seemed to drink in her features with a deep pos-
sessiveness.

Gently, Lucas raised his hands to cup her face. It
seemed a long time before he found the words he
wanted. "Things won't ever be the same between us
again. You know that, don't you, Jessie?" he finally
grated heavily.

"Yes," she agreed very quietly. "I know that."

It was the truth and it was shattering. She had given
herself to this man completely. And for no other reason than that he had reached out to take her! He had
wanted her and had claimed her as if she were his by
right.

Even as he rolled reluctantly to one side and helped
her stumble awkwardly to her feet, Jessica began the

mental tirade she knew she would be castigating herself with for a long time to come. But nothing could change what had happened between them tonight. As long as she was a part of his small tribe, subject to his leadership, Jessica knew she would be his.

She winced as her bare foot encountered a small rock and then she submitted to being dressed by her lover. No, she thought dazedly, not my lover. The dominant male in the herd. I have given myself to the male who holds the most power in this corner of the world. What did that make her?

Lucas said little as he finished getting both of them dressed and then he pulled her close against his side and started back toward the campsite. Dazed and bemused, Jessica allowed herself to be guided along the edge of the stream. Although her mind was churning with the knowledge of what had happened, her body still remembered the lovemaking and it protested the exertion. Some small voice said she should be lying in Lucas's arms until morning, not going back to her own bed alone.

Just beyond the range of the nearly dead fire with its circle of sleeping people, Lucas drew her to a halt and turned her to face him. "Whatever happens now," he murmured deeply, "you belong to me." He bent his head to brush her lips.

She stared up at him wordlessly, knowing that for the duration of the ordeal she had no choice. In this time and in this place she did, indeed, belong to him.

He released her then, returning her to the cushions that were her bed and making his way back to his own. Across the glowing embers that were all that remained of the fire, his eyes met hers as they both settled beneath makeshift blankets. Knowing herself hunted and trapped, Jessica stifled a cry deep in her throat and turned to bury her face in the cushion. She could no longer meet the masculine possession in that steady gray gaze. Morning became a time to dread....

But the brilliant glow of a desert dawn brought with it the distant drone of an aircraft engine. For Jessica there was no time to think about what had happened during the night. She joined the others as they slowly awakened to the import of the plane. In taut silence the sleepy passengers sat up in their makeshift beds one by one, staring up at the pearl-bright sky.

Lucas spoke first, glancing over at Gary. "They'll hit the ELT signal any minute now."

Gary exchanged a man-to-man glance with him as he sat erect amid his array of cushions and clothes. "None too soon, either."

Sensing the undercurrent of grim understanding that was running between the two men, Jessica stared from one to the other. "What do you mean?" she asked.

Lucas shrugged, his gaze shifting to her questioning face. "The ELT runs on batteries. The signal doesn't go on forever," he replied simply.

"How long?" she managed tensely, as it began to dawn on her that the instrument in which they had all put so much trust might not have been infallible after all.

"Six to eight days maximum for that model in the Otter," Gary told her ruefully.

He had the full attention of the group now. Mabel stared at him. "You mean Lucas and you knew there was a time limit on that device? And you didn't tell us?''

''Wasn't much point in scaring everyone,'' Lucas drawled firmly, throwing back his covers and surging lithely to his feet.

''Do you think my daddy will be in the plane?'' Matt inquired eagerly, leaping off his cushions excitedly. His question served to redirect the attention of the group and everyone once again stared skyward.

''If he's not in the plane, it's a sure bet he'll be waiting for you after the helicopter picks us up,'' Lucas assured the boy, ruffling the youngster's hair affectionately.

''Helicopter?'' Dave asked interestedly.

''That's about all they can use to get us out of this canyon,'' Gary responded seriously. ''It was a stroke of luck the Otter made it down in one piece. No reasonable pilot would try it if there were alternatives!''

''And here I was hoping they would send jeeps or mules at the very least!'' Jessica grumbled, getting stiffly to her feet. She hid a small wince at the unfamiliar twinges in her body. Souvenirs of last night, she thought wryly; memories of what it meant to be the only available female in a herd being dominated by a virile male. She bent down to fold clothing in an attempt to hide the rush of red into her cheeks.

''Why did you want them to send out jeeps or mules, Jessie?'' Sharon demanded.

''Because I have no desire to ever fly again!'' Jessica forced herself to retort with a grin at the little girl. ''I'll go out by helicopter if that's the only alternative, but after this, I'm sticking to ground transportation!''

"Nonsense," Gary groaned, his hand going to his head. "Don't you know statistics prove you're far safer in an airplane than you are in a car?"

"Statistics don't always outweigh emotions," Lucas put in wryly, his eyes seeking out Jessica's gaze. "I know how Jessie feels."

Before she was able to find a suitably light response, the approaching search plane swept overhead.

"They didn't see us!" Sharon yelped, stricken.

"They'll have the signal now," Lucas told her calmly. "The plane will be back. Just wait."

Sure enough, the increasing drone of the engine heralded another pass and this time the plane waggled its wingtips in recognition of their presence.

"Won't be long now," Gary sighed in satisfaction.

"Does this mean no more rabbit stew?" Abby chuckled as she climbed to her feet.

"This means Lucas has to start working on explanations to give his bunnies at the pet shop," Jessica couldn't resist putting in.

"I think I'll keep my murderous deeds a secret from them if possible," Lucas said dryly. "Something tells me they wouldn't understand."

The rescuing helicopter arrived two hours later. In the flurry and excitement of the operation, there was no time for Jessica to dwell on the events of the previous evening. She threw herself into preparations for being rescued with a vengeance, gathering up the various items of clothing and repacking the suitcases. As far as Sharon and Matt were concerned, they now regarded the whole event as a camping trip. Abby and Mabel expressed their relief in more subtle ways, but it was blatantly evident. Gary and Dave helped Lucas ensure that the fire was well and truly out.

In a way it *had* been a camping trip, Jessica reflected with a small, disbelieving shake of her head. No one had gone hungry and no one had gotten cold, thanks to Lucas. Everyone and everything was well organized and ready for the helicopter, but no one ran forward with cries of relief when it landed. The happiness was genuine but not hysterical. There was an unspoken knowledge that they could have held out much longer for rescue if it had been necessary. They all boarded rather sedately.

Jessica, seated in the noisy craft, saw the nod of cool, male admiration the pilot gave Lucas as he came through the door last. The man had obviously assessed the difference between the morale and health of this group and others he had been obliged to assist during the years and knew with unerring instinct who was responsible for it. Lucas took a seat beside Jessica as the 'copter lifted back off the canyon floor. She was eternally grateful that the roar of whirling blades made it impossible to talk.

Matt's and Sharon's daddy wasn't the only one waiting when the helicopter set down on the tarmac of the small desert town from which the search crews had been dispatched. The children's mother was also there, the quarrel with her husband evidently forgotten, at least for the duration of the ordeal. The two ran forward to embrace their laughing, excited offspring.

Abby and Mabel found an entire entourage of senior citizens, all friends, plus two generations of family gathered in the glaring heat of the sun. Dave was met by his father, a tall man with the carriage of a retired military officer, who greeted his son with barely disguised emotion.

No one came running forward to meet Lucas and as she walked beside him toward the small waiting room, Jessica realized that until that moment she hadn't even considered the possibility that he might have been married. Was the rush of relief she now experienced only because she wouldn't have to feel guilty about having slept with a married man?

"No family here to greet you?" he asked quietly, surveying the crowd waiting at the gate.

"Scanlon will undoubtedly have sent someone," she returned calmly, searching the sea of faces.

"The hotel is your family?" He smiled wryly.

"I'm afraid so. My parents died several years ago and I don't have any close relatives," she told him honestly. "What about you?"

"Similar sob story, I'm afraid," he chuckled. "I doubt the bunnies sent anyone."

That brought a smile to her lips and Jessica's eyes sparkled for a moment in genuine humor and warmth. But before she could say anything, the crowd, consisting mostly of reporters, as it turned out, was upon them.

"Jessie! Jessie! Over here!"

She turned her head at the shouted greeting, recognizing Lee Simon's worried face. The handsome man in the three-piece suit hurried forward. Behind him, parked at the curb, Jessica could see a waiting black limousine with a chauffeur standing nearby.

"Scanlon always does things with style," she had

time to tell Lucas as Simon made his way through the throng of reporters and television crews. "Lee manages a resort hotel not far from here."

"I see." Lucas was ignoring the barrage of questions being aimed his way as he watched Lee Simon greet Jessica with restrained enthusiasm.

"Thank God you're all right, Jessie! Scanlon management has been deeply worried, I assure you!"

"Afraid the convention plans for the next twelve months were going to disintegrate without me to supervise them?" she teased, grateful for the greeting, even if it wasn't quite the same as having a real family member present.

"There were dire rumors to the effect that, if anything permanent had happened to you, I was going to have to fill your shoes!" Lee grinned. "God! I can't believe it! We were all so damned scared! Listen, I've got a car waiting as soon as the authorities turn you loose. I'm taking you straight back to the resort. Scanlon management left strict instructions for you to rest for two weeks before even thinking about going back to work!"

"Thanks, Lee, I intend to do exactly that!"

"You all look fairly healthy," broke in an urgent voice at her elbow. She turned to see a reporter thrusting a microphone in her face. "In fact none of you really seems to need a rest cure! How did it go out there, Miss Travers?"

Aware of Lucas standing close at her side, Jessica remembered her duty to the Scanlon hotel chain. If she was to be a source of publicity for them, she must handle it adroitly.

"We're all in excellent shape, Mr. Richardson," she announced calmly, reading the man's name tag as she spoke. "Thanks to Lucas Kincaid. Mr. Kincaid here was in charge the entire time. We all owe him our lives."

That was all it took to send the reporters swarming over Lucas. Jessica watched him virtually disappear in a sea of microphones and recording machines. Then she realized that this was her chance.

"Take me away from here, Lee," she whispered gruffly. "I'll talk to the authorities later if necessary. I just want to get away."

"You bet," he agreed instantly, taking her elbow. "Right this way, Jessie. I can't wait to get to a phone to let everyone know you're really okay."

She moved off with him, Lucas lost in the crowd behind her. She had no way of knowing, of course, how he intended to treat her now that they were safely back in civilization. Perhaps he would have lost interest immediately. Or perhaps he would have pursued her in an attempt to reestablish his claim. Either way, she knew she must escape. The memory of the past five days would be difficult enough to handle as it was.

Safe in the cushioned luxury of the air-conditioned limousine, Jessica settled back into the seat with a sigh. No, she never wanted to see Lucas Kincaid again. The man had stripped away the trappings of her sophisticated, polished world, humiliating her by forcing her to submit to his authority in front of the others and then reducing her to the status of a primitive female animal in his arms. Last night, she told herself again and again, should never have happened. She would never forgive herself for allowing it to occur. As if she'd had any choice in the matter!

That last thought brought a wave of color into her cheeks and she sat staring sightlessly out the window at the dry landscape. Lucas Kincaid had approached her on the most primitive of levels and she had accepted his right to do so. She was furious and disgusted with herself. No, she never wanted to see the man again.

Three

Three days later, Jessica surged up through the sun-warmed water of the cruise ship's pool with a feeling of incredible exhilaration. A two-week cruise from Los Angeles to Mexico, courtesy of Scanlon Hotels! No one could say her company didn't have a heart, she thought, smiling to herself as she tossed back the wet tendrils of tawny hair and braced herself lightly at the edge of the pool.

It seemed that management couldn't bring itself to believe that five days spent surviving a plane crash in a desert canyon wouldn't exhaust one of its prized executives. She had been offered the choice of two weeks in one of Scanlon's luxurious hotels on the coast or the cruise to Mexico. Knowing that she'd only end up working if she went to one of the hotels, Jessica had opted for the first available cruise.

Today was the first day of the voyage. The elegant

white ship had set out with a full quota of eager passengers and a good number of them, like Jessica, had already made their way to one of the two pools on board.

Water dripped from the sleek lines of the brilliant persimmon swimsuit with its halter neckline and high-on-the-thigh cut as Jessica climbed the ladder at the edge of the pool. At one end of the pool a convenient bar was already crowded with a variety of passengers in bare feet and sunclothes. Catching up the full-sized white bathsheet which had the words "Scanlon Hotels" woven into the nap of the fabric, she quickly brushed the water from her skin and headed toward the outdoor bar.

More than one man hovering on a barstool watched her approach. Jessica ignored them, aware that they were assessing everything that went by in a swimsuit that afternoon. Sinking into one of the webbed chairs beside a small table, Jessie ordered a glass of iced tea from the white-uniformed steward who hurried toward her.

When it arrived, it was not brought by the steward. Jessica glanced up, one eyebrow arched inquiringly, a cool smile on her lips as a man who had been seated at the bar delivered the drink with a flourish.

"I hope you don't mind. I took the liberty of having it put on my tab. I'm Kirk Randall." The man's blue eyes, set in a handsome, tennis-tanned face beneath stylishly windblown near-blond hair, smiled down at her.

Jessica hesitated and then shrugged. "Thank you,"

she said demurely, accepting the glass and, in so doing, his presence. "Jessica Travers. Call me Jessie."

"I was thinking of calling you a fellow hotel towel
thief." Kirk grinned, sitting down beside her with
alacrity. He was wearing monogrammed white shorts
and a red polo shirt with a horrid little animal embroidered on the left breast. Combined with the fashionable deck shoes, his attire and manner spelled politely stated success. He was probably in his early
thirties, Jessica guessed as he nodded at her white
bathsheet.

"I'm afraid my collection of stolen towels is limited
to those with 'Scanlon' on them," she chuckled.

"Specializing?"

"Only the best. I have an inside track, though. I
work for the chain."

"That definitely gives you an unfair edge," Kirk
complained good-naturedly. "I have to work much
harder to collect mine. Are you, uh, traveling alone?"

No sense wasting time, is there? Jessica asked silently. Then she smiled. "Yes. I'm recuperating," she
added dryly.

"Nothing serious, I hope."

"An unscheduled landing in a desert canyon."

Kirk snapped his fingers as if something had clicked
mentally. "I thought you looked vaguely familiar!
That little commuter plane that went down in the desert a few days ago? You and some others were
stranded for four or five days, weren't you? Saw you
on T.V. just before you climbed into a car and were
whisked away."

"Scanlon takes good care of its own," she murmured, sipping at the iced tea. "I was protected from publicity and reporters until I could be ushered quietly on board this ship. By the time we get back to L.A. everyone will have forgotten about the whole thing."

"I won't mention it to anyone else. What a hell of an experience it must have been, though," Kirk said, shaking his head in awe.

"You know what they say about landings," Jessica quipped. "Any one you can walk away from is a good one!" The words reminded her of Lucas's reassurance to the co-pilot and that, in turn, reminded her that the real reason she had let Scanlon protect her from publicity was that she wanted to stay hidden from Lucas Kincaid.

Lee Simon had arranged to keep her incognito at his resort for the first twenty-four hours after the return to civilization and then he had turned her over to others from Scanlon, who had sheltered her in privacy at one of the coastal hotels. Jessica would never really know if Lucas had made any attempt to find her, but she had considered it prudent to take precautions. The feeling of running scared was a new and unwelcome one to her, but she was intelligent enough to obey her instincts. And they all screamed "run."

"Have you arranged your dinner seating?" Kirk inquired politely.

"I'll be eating at the second seating. I figure I'll need the extra time to work off all the rest of the food they serve during the day," she said smiling.

"I mean, have you arranged to share your table with anyone in particular?" he asked carefully.

"No, I said I'd be glad to mix and mingle," Jessica

said with a determined airiness. Kirk Randall seemed nice enough, but the last thing she wanted to do on this voyage was tie herself to any one person for the duration of the trip.

"Well, it's probably too late to do anything about this evening, but perhaps tomorrow night we can arrange to be seated at the same table," Kirk went on hopefully.

"We'll see."

The dress Jessica chose for dinner that night was a flamboyant statement of her intention to have fun on the cruise. In red silk, it was bare at the top, ruffled at the knee-length, diagonal hem and wrapped at the hip for a dramatic effect of which she was totally aware. She paired it with strappy red heels and dangling red-and-white earrings. Then she pulled her hair into a severe knot at the nape of her neck which set off the strong, feminine lines of her face to perfection. There was nothing soft or submissive in the overall look she had achieved, Jessica told herself as she took one last look in the mirror. Instead there was sophistication, poise, and cool control sparked with a flare of independence. She nodded decisively, satisfied. Definitely not a herd doe waiting to be singled out and overcome by the head buck!

That analogy made her cringe and she turned away from her image, firmly repressing her self-disgust. She would never see Lucas Kincaid again. Now all she had to do was make herself forget what he had done to her. And the best way to forget that was to throw herself into the shipboard fun and games.

The elegant dining room was a sea of gleaming

crystal, snowy tablecloths, and silver with the cruise line's crest engraved on it. White-jacketed stewards stood at the ready as the passengers who had elected the second seating filed into the paneled room. Jessica found her table readily and greeted the middle-aged couple who had already been seated there. With a friendly smile she took her seat and wondered who would be the fourth at the small table.

Around her the beautifully dressed diners assumed seats, and a pleasant hum of conversation filled the room. Jessica turned to the couple beside her and began an introductory conversation. One thing about being in the hotel business, she thought, one learned how to talk to strangers!

"This is our first cruise," Mrs. Howard confided after introductions had been made. "Bill and I have been promising it to ourselves for years. Finally, this year I told him we were going to stop putting it off!"

"Good idea." Jessica agreed and reached for the menu in front of her plate.

"Are you traveling alone?" the balding Mr. Howard inquired politely as he, too, reached for a menu.

"Yes. I'm taking a vacation. Will you just look at all this food! Knowing it's already been paid for in the cruise fare makes for a terrible temptation to have something from every category, doesn't it? Normally I would never think of ordering an appetizer and a salad and a soup and an entrée and dessert and cheese!"

Ann Howard chuckled delightedly. "We'd heard about the quantity of food we'd be receiving on board, so Bill and I took off five pounds during the past month getting ready.''

Jessica laughed. ''Smart thinking. I'll just have to make up my mind to take off the five pounds *after* we return to L.A.!''

''I wonder where our fourth is at this table?'' Ann remarked, glancing around.

''Perhaps there isn't one.'' Jessica shrugged, trying to choose between the raw marinated squid and the escargot from the list of appetizers. Squid sounded good.

''Perhaps not,'' Ann agreed slowly and then brightened as she glanced toward the dining room entrance. ''Oh, that must be him now. He's heading this way. How lucky! Another man for this table!''

Jessica glanced up automatically and abruptly the choice between squid and escargot was rendered insignificant. Lucas Kincaid was gliding purposefully across the room, his gray eyes watching her with unwavering intent.

Jessica's fingers clenched the little menu in her hand with a fierceness that wrinkled it as she watched the approach of the man with the jungle-cat hair. Her mind was a sudden whirl of chaotic reaction. Anger, fear, and dread were all mixed into the witch's brew of her emotions. Her first instinct was to run and then her blazing fury took over, keeping her firmly in her seat.

She was back in civilization now. This man no longer had any power over her. She repeated the litany again and again as Lucas came toward the table.

Unlike the other men in the room, who were wearing expensive evening jackets or dashing blazers, Lu-

cas had on a fawn-colored corduroy jacket, which
looked as if it had seen better days. The button-down
shirt was of cotton instead of a more elegant fabric
and the plain, dark tie appeared to be about two years
out of style. The slacks, which fit his lean body well
enough, were of an inexpensive polyester blend and
Jessica could have sworn the low, worn boots he had
on were the same ones he'd been wearing the day of
the crash. Quite suddenly, as she sat there in her sophisticated red silk dress, Jessica began to regain a
measure of her self-control. Lucas Kincaid had fit the
rough desert scene quite well. In fact, he had dominated it. But here among the expensively attired cruise
passengers, he looked out of place and out of his element.

It was that knowledge that enabled Jessica to meet
his eyes as he came to a halt, one strong, short-nailed
hand on the back of the vacant chair across from her.

"Hello, Jessie," he said with a smoothness which
didn't quite mask the gravel in his voice. "It's lucky
for me you picked a ship, isn't it? Chasing you from
one Scanlon hotel to another for the past three days
has been something of a chore. At least here you can't
run any farther than the end of the boat!"

The color washed out of her face and then surged
back, a mingling of fury and determination to maintain
her control at all costs. "Hello, Lucas. I would have
thought you'd have been busy putting down a bunny
rebellion during the past few days, not chasing after
me," she said very carelessly.

That took him back. The dark lashes lowered, hood-
ing the iron-gray eyes speculatively. He had grown

accustomed to her obedience, she realized with soaring pleasure. Lucas hadn't been expecting flippancy. Slowly he sat down, his gaze never leaving her serenely controlled features.

"I couldn't think of a good enough story to give the bunnies. It seemed safer to go after you, instead," he surprised her by saying calmly.

Ann Howard interrupted cheerfully. "Oh, how wonderful! You two know each other. I'm Ann Howard and this is my husband, Bill. Who are you and how do you happen to know Jessie, here?"

Lucas tore his eyes away from Jessie's face and managed a small smile for Ann Howard and her husband. "Lucas Kincaid. Jessie and I met a few days ago. We, uh, got separated before we could finish some business we had started. I was lucky enough to learn she was scheduled to be on this cruise."

"Lucky?" Jessica drawled, her voice implying that she thought luck had probably had little to do with his finding her.

His eyes swung back to her. "Let's just say Scanlon employees don't come cheap. I'm going to have to sell an unbelievable number of parakeets and tropical fish to cover the cost of the bribe I was forced to use!"

"Who did you bribe?" she inquired with acid sweetness.

"Why? You want to thank him?"

"I'll have his job when I return!" she shot back grimly.

He nodded, picking up his menu. "You'd do that, wouldn't you? I've learned a lot about you in the past few days, Jessie. You're very high up in the Scanlon chain, aren't you? You hold a great deal of authority."

"You were fortunate in being able to get a place on this cruise on such short notice," Bill Howard put in, clearly feeling some responsibility to lighten the atmosphere. "Wasn't it sold out?"

"There are always a few cancellations at the last minute, I guess. Since I didn't have the clout of Scanlon behind me when I booked, I was, indeed, fortunate." The iron eyes glittered as Lucas lifted his gaze to look at Jessica over the top of his menu.

He wasn't really furious, she decided, avoiding his accusing glare, just annoyed with her. That gave her one more psychological edge. Her emotions were far more violent!

The steward appeared at their table a moment later, saving Jessica from having to make further conversation. "I'll have the squid, the broccoli and red pepper salad, a small bowl of gazpacho soup and the veal with mushrooms," she ordered briskly when her turn came. Damned if she would let Lucas's presence ruin her meal!

"And for dessert?" the steward prompted helpfully.

"Well, I was going to have both the chocolate soufflé and the selection of cheeses, but I think I'll just have the cheese," she decided slowly.

"Very good." The man nodded. "And you, sir?" He turned to Lucas, who smiled wryly. "A steak and salad, please. With a baked potato on the side. Oh, and I'll try the chocolate soufflé she just turned down."

"I'm with you," Bill announced. "A good steak

suits me just fine any day. Ann and I aren't all that adventurous in our eating habits, I guess. Soup, salad, and steak. Sounds good.'' He handed over the menu with satisfaction as his wife nodded in agreement.

"Would you care for wine?" the steward inquired before taking his leave. Having summed up the culinary expertise at the table, he turned to Jessica as he spoke. So did the others. Feeling three sets of eyes on her, as well as those of the steward, Jessica dutifully chose a soft French burgundy she hoped the others would enjoy.

The dinner conversation went rather well, all things considered, thanks chiefly to the cheerful enthusiasm of Bill and Ann. Jessica ate her food with a relish that surprised her. Perhaps it was because the more exotic fare put one more subtle barrier between herself and Lucas. Out on the desert the basics might assume monumental importance, she told herself with an air of superiority, but here in the civilized world there was room for the finer things of life. She fully intended to enjoy them. Let Lucas eat steak and salad; she had learned to appreciate more interesting food! And the marinated raw squid tasted even better than usual.

It wasn't until she had eaten the last bite of rich Stilton cheese and realized the Howards were rising and preparing to leave that Jessica allowed herself to worry about what happened next. She caught the anticipatory gleam in Lucas's gray eyes and knew he was readying himself for a private confrontation. She had learned to read him well out there on the desert. There was no doubt but that he was going to make an attempt now to corner her.

Well, she wasn't going to sit around and wait for him to pounce! Getting quickly to her feet, Jessica smiled aloofly at the others. "I shall see you tomorrow morning at breakfast," she said politely to Bill and Ann.

"Maybe we'll run into the two of you in one of the lounges later on this evening," Ann responded warmly, glancing at Lucas as she spoke.

"Perhaps," Jessica said dryly, turning on her heel to sweep out of the dining room in a flounce of polished red silk. Her mind was made up before she reached the door. A stroll on one of the decks should serve to separate her sufficiently from Lucas. It was, after all, a big ship.

The thought that what she was doing was tantamount to running away flickered through her mind more than once, but Jessica pushed it aside. She needed a little time to think.

Lucas, however, chose not to allow her that time. He caught up with her just as she stepped outside into the balmy night air.

"A little like a night back on the desert, isn't it?" he inquired quietly as he loomed up behind her and took her elbow.

Jessica's anger and fear flared with unexpected force as she felt the strength in the hand on her arm. "No, Lucas, it's not at all like a night out on the desert," she hissed, halting to face him. "It's another world entirely. My world. And in my world you don't have any right to hound me like this! In my world you don't have any rights over me at all!"

He sighed, forcing her gently over to the railing. "I had a feeling you were going to be madder than hell."

"What did you expect?" she demanded stiffly, gazing out to sea as he lounged against the rail on one elbow and studied her tense profile. "If the situation had been reversed, how would you be feeling?"

"I can't imagine the situation in reverse," he admitted honestly.

"You can only see it from a man's point of view, is that it?"

"I am a man." He shrugged. "How else could I see it?"

Jessica heard the quiet, masculine statement of fact and shut her eyes briefly against the impossibility of ever making him understand. Then she opened them very wide and turned to look at him. "Given that insurmountable barrier," she began with emphatic steadiness, "I can only try to spell out my position very slowly and carefully and hope you can find some method of comprehending matters."

"I don't think I want to hear this."

"Your only option is to turn around and walk away. I'm flexible. If you choose that alternative I will understand!"

"After that first day on the desert you didn't yell at me like this," he complained gently.

"I am not yelling! Listen to me, Lucas," she said tightly. "I meant what I said. What happened after the crash occurred in another time and in another place. I'm home now and back to operating under my own rules, not those of some self-appointed master who thinks he has the right to take what he wants."

He nodded morosely, staring down at the foaming wake of the ship far below. "I was afraid it might take you a while to get over that little scene we went through after the landing. I knew at the time that you weren't used to taking orders and I've learned since then that you're very accustomed to giving them. It must have been difficult for you, but you're intelligent enough to realize I didn't have much choice, Jessie."

Her fingers tightened on the railing, the knuckles going white. "That *little* scene, as you so lightly put it, was only the beginning, Lucas Kincaid," she blazed fiercely. "It's going to take me a while to get over it, all right, a *long* while. But I just might manage it, eventually. I will never believe it was necessary, however. Things could have been settled between us privately, away from the others. We could have formed a leadership team, taking advantage of each other's expertise."

"Damn it, Jessie! That wasn't management training school out there! It wasn't the kind of position in which you can experiment with new theories of leadership! At least admit that the plan I instituted had the virtue of working!"

"It worked," she allowed coolly. "I'll give you that much. But don't expect me to thank you for making a fool out of me in front of six other people, and don't expect me to forgive you for the way you assumed that winning that battle gave you the right to watch me bathing, or the right to force yourself on me!"

He looked up quickly, eyes narrowing in sudden understanding. "Oh, my God," he muttered disgustedly. "So that's it. You're equating your surrender to my authority with your surrender later in my arms."

"The fact that you even use words like *surrender* to describe both instances shows how impossible it will be for us to ever establish any kind of reasonable relationship. You've wasted your time and money coming along on this cruise, Lucas Kincaid. You no longer have any rights or any power over me, do you understand? I'm not going to follow meekly as you lead me off to bed!"

"The way you did last time?" he drawled with a crooked little grin.

She looked away from the memories in those gray eyes, infuriated with herself for even bothering with the discussion. "Leave me alone, Lucas."

"I can't," he said starkly, the small grin fading as he watched her face. "I want you. You belong to me, sweetheart," he added almost gently. "And I think you know it. Do you really expect me to walk away and leave you alone?"

"Is it so hard for pet shop owners to find female companionship, then?" she challenged, appalled at his claim and just as appalled at the way she had been expecting it.

"I imagine it's tough for any man to find the right woman," Lucas acknowledged blandly. "But when he does he'd be a complete fool to let her go, wouldn't he?"

Jessica spun around to lean against the rail with all the mocking nonchalance she could muster. Arrogantly she let her eyes rove over his lean, unfashionably dressed frame. "What in hell," she asked softly, "makes you think I'm the right woman for you?"

His face hardened at the icy condescension in her words, but he undertook to answer the question. "You think the fact that you have chic, sophisticated clothes, or the fact that you order things like marinated squid instead of steak makes any real difference? Don't forget, lady, I've seen the other side of you. I've seen you get up half a dozen times in the middle of the night to check an injured man's pulse and soothe a worried kid. I've seen you wash clothes in a stream and I've seen you amuse an elderly lady by playing a game of checkers in the sand with pebbles for markers. I've also seen you looking dirty and disheveled and fighting mad but able to surrender gracefully when your common sense told you it was for the best. And last, but not least, I've known what it's like to hold you in my arms and have you give yourself completely to me when I needed you more than I've ever needed any woman in my life. Oh, yes, Jessie Travers. You're the right woman for me. Whether you realize it seems to be an issue at the moment, but I'll make sure you do before this cruise is over!"

"Your caveman tactics won't work on board this ship, Lucas!" But at the bottom of her defiance, Jessica could feel the rush of fear. He had mastered her so easily less than a week ago!

"I don't see why not. They worked once before!" His annoyance flared briefly as he reacted to the rebellion in her. "Oh, hell, Jessie," he went on disgustedly. "Don't make me say things I don't mean!"

Jessica found herself strangely gratified at the slip

in his composure. Very slowly but steadily she was convincing her senses of what her mind already knew to be true: She *was* safe on this ship. Quite out of his reach. It was good to see the growing frustration in him, she realized. She wanted him to know that what had happened after the plane crash had been an aberration in her behavior. She would never again play the weak, submissive role to his dominant, aggressive one.

"I think you meant what you just said," she stated evenly. "Why not? It's the truth. Your tactics did work in that particular situation. What you're going to have to learn, Lucas, is that such situations do not constitute a normal way of life for me! It is highly unlikely that you and I will ever find ourselves in such circumstances again."

He looked at her for a long moment. "You're telling me that it takes such dramatic circumstances to release the softer side of your nature?" he finally asked silkily.

Jessica flushed. "I do not consider what happened an example of the softer side of my nature," she bit out. "I consider it an example of the primitive, female animal side of my nature!"

"You're ashamed of your behavior, aren't you?" he demanded gently. "Ashamed of not doing a better job of standing up to me immediately after the crash and ashamed of the way you gave yourself to me that night. Jessie, you've got it all wrong in your head, you little idiot! Let me show you that everything is the same between us and always will be regardless of the circumstances or the surroundings—"

She stepped back with the movement of a startled cat as he reached out, her aquamarine eyes widening with fear. When his hands fell back to his sides, Jessica forced herself to relax. He wouldn't dare try to force himself on her here, she thought. He wouldn't *dare!*

"I told you those tactics won't work," she told him with a spirited rush of confidence. "You can't just reach out and take what you want this time, Lucas."

He swore softly. "You make it sound as if you were some helpless, mindless creature I used for my own pleasure. Is that the way it was, Jessie? Are you going to stand there and tell me you would have let any man make love to you in those circumstances? Are you going to claim you would have let any male lead you off into the sand the way I did that night? Would you really have given yourself so completely to just *any* man who asked it of you the way I did?"

When Jessica flinched he relentlessly pursued his advantage, subtly closing the small gap between them at the rail. "What about it, Jessie? Going to say you were so browbeaten you would have let whichever male happened to be in charge take advantage of you?"

It was too much. Jessica lost her temper and her self-control in a flash of sheer fury. Her palm lashed out, hitting the side of his face with branding force.

For an instant stunned silence hung heavily between the two rigid figures on the deck. For her part Jessica knew an instinctive urge to run as if her life depended on it. But pride made flight impossible. Instead she faced the iron-eyed man who stood staring down at her in anger.

Eventually Lucas spoke, his fingers lifting gingerly to his reddened cheek. The tension seemed to fade a little from the lean lines of his body. "I deserved that, I suppose. My only excuse was that I was losing my temper rapidly."

"I noticed," she remarked scathingly. But her courage was flooding back as she realized he wasn't going to retaliate. "One of the many advantages of being back in civilization," she went on sweetly, "is that I don't have to fear your temper."

A slow, rueful smile unexpectedly touched the corners of his mouth. "Meaning you wouldn't have dared try that little stunt if we were still stranded out in the desert?"

Jessica lifted one shoulder in seemingly casual dismissal, a feeling of being back on top of the situation coming over her. "I would have been too terrified of cutting off the supply of rabbits."

"Well at least you had more sense than to bite the hand that fed you," he allowed, his expression softening with wry humor.

Jessica lifted her chin firmly. "In any event the situation won't arise again. History isn't likely to repeat itself. You shouldn't have come after me, Lucas."

"I had no choice," he said simply. "I want you."

Restlessly, her body reacting uneasily to his words, Jessica moved one hand in an impatient arc. "What do you want from me? An affair? Is that what you need to satisfy your ego?"

"Will you give me that much?" he countered almost whimsically.

"No!"

"You're really scared of me, aren't you?" he muttered, shaking his head in disbelief. "Jessie, that's idiotic. You can't go on holding what happened a week ago against me!"

"I don't see why not," she tossed back gamely.

"Honey, it's yourself you're trying to punish. Don't you see? I think the reason you're so angry is because during those few days you were forced into a role that revealed a side of your nature you've tried to conceal. I told you I've been learning something about you during the past few days as I chased you from one hotel to another. You're smart, you're aggressive, you've got a lot of natural authority that you've channeled into a successful career with Scanlon. Everyone I met admires you and respects you. They're also a little in awe of you, a little wary. I think for the most part they would obey you in a crisis—right down to the last man in the last ditch. You're a natural leader. But I think that none of the people I talked to has ever seen the other side of your nature. You've kept that well concealed, haven't you? To make it in a man's world you had to keep it repressed. But back in the desert I gave you no choice except to make a different kind of contribution to the group."

Jessica caught her breath. "Thank you for the elementary analysis. I'm sure you'll understand if I don't put a lot of faith in the psychoanalytical capabilities of a pet shop owner! Go home and try your skills on a parakeet!"

He grimaced. "I didn't learn my analysis techniques running the pet shop," he admitted ruefully. "I learned them in a much more instructive environment!"

She blinked in surprise, unable to stifle the deep curiosity which sprang to life at his words. Before Jessica could stop herself, she was asking the inevitable question. "Where did you learn them?"

"In the streets of L.A. I was with the LAPD for eight years," he sighed, glancing down again at the foaming water far below.

"The Los Angeles Police Department? You were a cop?" she asked, astonished.

"A classic case of job burnout," he told her, his mouth skewing wryly. "Eight years of dealing with L.A. crazies and street gangs was enough to convince me I needed a career change! I got out before the job got me."

"I see," she whispered slowly. It explained a lot, Jessica thought wonderingly. It explained his tough, take-charge attitude when the chips were down and it probably explained why he thought himself qualified to analyze her behavior. An L.A. cop undoubtedly picked up a lot of basic psychology in the streets. Or *thought* he did!

"But I don't come from that world, Lucas. I come from a much more civilized, more sophisticated environment. You can't apply what you learned there to me."

"Jessie, you can't ignore what happened between us!"

"I don't see why not!"

"Damn it! I'll show you why not!" He moved, then, coming away from the rail with the effortless swiftness of a gray-eyed leopard. She was in his arms before she had time to realize she was trapped.

Four

The sweeping impact of his embrace riveted Jessica's senses. She stood perfectly still beneath the onslaught, her fingers splayed against his chest. Lucas caught her mouth as it was turned upward, lips slightly parted in astonishment. The small cry of protest was stifled in her throat.

The first impression that roared through Jessica's mind was that this kiss was from a different end of the spectrum than the ones to which she had been exposed that night in the desert. That night there had been primitive seduction and need blended with the mastery and demand. Tonight the attempt at mastery was washing out everything else.

It was as if Lucas had tired of trying to talk her back into his arms and had opted for a more direct approach. Which was, Jessica knew, precisely the case.

Initially he didn't ask for a response. Instead he seemed intent on restaking the claim he felt he'd made a few nights previously. His hands locked against the red silk dress as he pulled her firmly into place against the hardening line of his body.

When Jessica resisted, he swung halfway around, setting his back against the rail, legs braced aggressively apart. Then he propelled her intimately between the strength of his thighs so that she was off balance and cradled in the heat of him.

Through the thin silk material of her dress, Jessica was made violently aware of the arousal Lucas had no intention of concealing. He wanted her to know, wanted her to feel the masculine challenge with every fiber of her body.

The stars began to spin overhead and the gentle, rhythmic motion of the huge ship threatened to sweep Jessica into a sensuous pattern that was as old as the sea itself.

Lucas dampened her lips with the aggressive tip of his tongue and when she once again tried to make a muffled sound of protest, he seized the opportunity to swiftly invade the territory he had once before conquered so thoroughly. Jessica trembled as he established a surging, thrusting cadence within her mouth that imitated the authority with which the ship plowed through the soft swells of the Pacific.

But no ship could totally conquer the sea, she told herself fleetingly. And here with the lights and sounds of seven hundred passengers nearby, she was safe. She was safe.

That knowledge blunted the arrow of fear and wariness, which would have caused her to struggle more violently. Instead, Jessica leaned passively against him, feeling his hands begin to slide along her spine up to the bareness at her shoulders and then back to the sensitive area at the base. Her short nails sank into the fabric of the corduroy jacket with the force of little claws as her entire body began to search for something it had once known there in Lucas's arms.

"Jessie, Jessie, please don't put up unnecessary barriers between us," he ground out raggedly as he reluctantly lifted his mouth a fraction of an inch from hers. "I'll only have to tear them down and it's such a waste of time!"

"The barriers are real," she managed throatily, trying to recover from the whirling vertigo his kiss had induced. "I only want to forget everything that happened back there in the desert. Can't you understand that? I don't want to think about how I let you humiliate me, even if it did assist in my own survival! I don't want to think about the way you made me feel like a cornered doe who belongs by right to the strongest male in the herd."

"That's not the way it was!"

"That's the way I remember it!" she flung back angrily.

Instead of arguing, he sealed her mouth once more beneath his own, but this time, as if the earlier kiss had assuaged some of his immediate hunger, he let his lips move slowly, invitingly on hers. Jessica felt the deliberate seduction and knew that it was far more dangerous than the attempt at dominance.

When several happy passengers spilled out of the

doorway and onto the open deck behind her, she knew she would have to take advantage of the opportunity to escape. Lucas slackened his grasp as the laughter and the good-natured comments filtered through the balmy night. His head came up slowly, freeing her mouth. When she began to pull away, he let her go, but in the process his hands slid around her rib cage, momentarily gliding possessively across her unconfined breasts.

Jessica stepped back hurriedly at the intimate touch. Her mouth was sensuously softened by his kisses. Her body tingled warmly where he had touched it and even the peak of her breast was tautening beneath the soft red silk. She knew he must have felt the budding nipple when he'd lightly passed his hand across her softness.

For a long moment they stared at each other in the shadows and Jessica knew well the memories in the gray eyes. She was very much afraid they were reflected in her own.

"You should never have come after me, Lucas," she admonished uneasily; then she turned on her heel and moved swiftly away toward the reassuring sounds of laughter and music drifting out to the deck from one of the three lounges.

Jessica threw herself into the darkened, smoky room, the red flounce of her dress swirling around her knees. Her eyes scanned the interior, searching for a vacant table. At the far end a small musical group energetically turned out dance music for the couples crowding the dance floor. A huge, circular padded bar dominated the opposite end of the room.

Concerned with the possibility that Lucas would pursue her and try to commandeer a few dances, Jessica turned toward the right, seeking some refuge in the boisterous crowd. She nearly collided with Kirk Randall, who was wearing a white evening jacket and well-tailored dark trousers. He looked every inch the elegantly casual cruise passenger, she thought fleetingly, remembering Lucas's rather battered corduroy jacket.

"I've been looking for you. How about dancing off some of that dinner? Or didn't you give in to the temptation to sample something from every section of the menu?" he grinned.

"Guilty as charged." Jessica fixed her most charming smile on her face and let him take her hand to lead her out onto the dance floor.

"I wasn't sure if you were going to end up spending the evening with that guy I saw seated at your table," Kirk remarked as he drew her into his arms. "Am I wrong or does his face seem familiar, too? Sorry," he added quickly when Jessica glanced up quizzically. "I'm one of those unlucky folks blessed with a memory for faces!"

"I'm afraid you probably saw Lucas in some of the same pictures where you saw me," she admitted with a smile. "He seems to have opted for a recuperative vacation, too."

"Kincaid, wasn't that the name?" When Jessica nodded mutely Kirk went on thoughtfully. "Quite a coincidence, his winding up on the same ship."

"Quite!"

"You two must, uh, have a lot to talk about," he suggested hesitantly.

"Not really," Jessica stated firmly. "Other than finding ourselves aboard the same ill-fated airplane, we have very little in common."

"Five days of being stranded together didn't provide enough fodder for conversation?" Kirk persisted quietly.

Jessica knew what he was getting at and her eyes hardened. "There were six other people around, Kirk. All the time."

He had the grace to redden slightly. "Sorry, I didn't mean to imply…"

"That we spent the five days making passionate love in the sand?" Damn! Why did she have to sound so defensive? Probably because it was too close to the truth.

"I guess the two of you really don't look like each other's type," Kirk allowed consideringly.

"We're not. Now if you don't mind, I'd rather not discuss him."

"My pleasure," he agreed readily and pulled her a little closer.

Jessica didn't spot Lucas in the lounge until after her second dance with Kirk and when she did it wasn't so much a case of spotting him as it was a feeling of awareness that prickled the skin at the nape of her neck. It was an irresistible, tingling sensation, which made her turn her head toward the far end of the crowded room, as Kirk walked her back to their small table. Lucas was at the bar, one elbow braced against

the upholstered edge, one heel hooked casually over a
rung of the stool he occupied with negligent ease.

He was watching her, a brooding expression in the
shadowed eyes which met hers across the intervening
space. He was nursing a glass of what looked like
bourbon and water. Even as Jessica's glance slid away
from his she saw the tall, attractive redhead slip gracefully onto the stool beside Lucas. A single man on
board a cruise ship was fair game.

When Jessica saw him again he was dancing with
the redhead. There was a slow, somewhat stilted style
to his movements that surprised her. It was not at all
the way she would have expected him to dance. Her
memories were of a lean, coordinated strength that
could master a woman in bed or on a dance floor. She
would have expected him to be a smooth, forceful
partner. Well, it was none of her business. Resolutely
she tried to pick up the thread of Kirk's polished conversation.

The next time Jessica happened to see Lucas in the
crowd, he was no longer with the redhead. A slightly
older, sophisticated blonde was in his arms on the
floor. The sight was oddly annoying.

As the evening progressed, Lucas appeared with one
new woman after another. Jessica knew that statisti-
cally women outnumbered men on most cruises, so it
was no wonder he seemed to have a wide choice of
dancing partners. Still, it was curious that he showed
no sign of settling down with any one woman for the
evening. Perhaps that rather stilted style he was ex-
hibiting was the reason!

"Looks like your friend is making up for his five

days of enforced abstinence in the desert," Kirk remarked with a small chuckle as he nodded in Lucas's direction.

Jessica ignored the comment and the warmth that washed up under her cheeks at the memory of at least one night that had not exactly been a model of abstinence. She made a subtle point of shifting her gaze derisively away from the sight of Lucas partnering a very determined-looking woman who seemed weighted down in Mexican silver jewelry and little else.

"If he doesn't make a choice fairly soon, he's going to wind up spending the night alone," Kirk went on knowingly.

"Meaning you don't intend to?" Jessica demanded coolly, her head coming around sharply in automatic hauteur.

"Take it easy," Kirk soothed. "I didn't mean..." He broke off abruptly as a strong, square hand descended on Jessica's shoulder.

"Excuse me," Lucas murmured. "I'd like to dance with Jessica." The iron eyes were on Kirk's, daring him to refuse permission. Under the branding touch of his hand, Jessica froze.

Then, when Kirk made the only possible response and nodded brusquely, she sighed inwardly and got slowly to her feet. Her mouth thinned in resigned acceptance of the situation, but there was nothing particularly resigned about the unexpected flutter in the pit of her stomach. As Lucas took her wrist and led her out onto the floor without a word, Jessica was unable to halt the rush of unwelcome fantasy. She remembered only too well how he had once led her just as silently away from the safety of camp and into a dangerous embrace.

The fantasy, unfortunately, was reinforced when Lucas drew her into his arms and wrapped her possessively close. There was none of the stiff formality in his dancing now. Jessica was molded into his warmth, left no option but to accept the sensuous glide of his body.

"If you go back to his stateroom tonight, I swear I'll throttle you, Jessie."

"Nothing like a bright, charming opening conversational gambit to set a pleasant mood on the dance floor, Lucas. Have you been using that line all evening?" she inquired frostily. "Perhaps that's the reason you haven't gotten any of your other dance partners to stick around for more than one number."

"Jessie, I'm not kidding. Your preppy friend is looking for an amusing bedmate tonight and that's all!"

"I tell great jokes in bed, Lucas," she dared in sugary, reassuring tones. "I know you didn't get a full sample of my bedroom wit because of the unusual circumstances in which we found ourselves last week, but don't worry. I do try to be amusing."

His fingers dug violently into her flesh through the thin material of the silk and Jessica sucked in her breath sharply.

"Honey, I know you're only trying to provoke me, but please use another technique. I can't guarantee I'll handle that one very well," he groaned.

Safe in the crowded room, feeling an irritation

which seemed to have its roots in the thought of all the women she had witnessed Lucas with that evening, Jessica purred mischievously, "I thought you could handle anything, Lucas."

He looked down at her, apparently attempting to analyze her mood. The note of caution in him was very welcome, Jessica decided. "I'm beginning to think life was simpler back there in the desert where you knew…" his voice trailed off.

"Where I knew and kept my place?" she concluded pertly, sea-green eyes gleaming now with poorly suppressed laughter. "But Lucas, I do know my place. And this time I'm going to maintain it. Out there on the desert the real problem was that I let you usurp my position. I let you put me in another place altogether. One I didn't care for and one I'll never accept again from any man!"

"Damn it, Jessie, will you stop harping on the past? I had no option last week but to do what was best for everyone. Let's just forget about it!" he snapped.

"Agreed," she drawled smoothly. "Consider it forgotten. That suits me just fine."

He stared at her warily before drawing a careful, steady breath. "Then we can start from scratch? Go on from here?"

"Why not?" She smiled brilliantly.

"Jessie, don't tease me," he growled warningly.

"I'm not. I'm willing to forget everything that happened a week ago."

He slid his hands up and down her slender back, sighing heavily with relief. Then he gently pushed her neat head down onto his shoulder. "Thank you, Jessie. It's going to be all right. I promise you."

"I'm sure it will be and now if you'll excuse me, the dance seems to be over and I must be getting back to Kirk." Her head popped up off his shoulder and her eyes burned brightly as she looked up at him.

Lucas stiffened as they came to a halt in the middle of the floor. "Jessie, I mean it! Don't tease me!" It was half a plea, half a warning.

"I wouldn't think of it. We're going to start over, remember? Pretend we've just met? You've danced one dance with every single woman in the room tonight, including me; now I must be getting back to my table. Thank you, Lucas."

She stepped away from him, but he caught her wrist. "You can't go back to him. He's only going to try to get you into his bed tonight."

"Why should you care? We've only just met. What possible difference could it make to you whom I spend the night with?" she mocked, waiting to spring her trap.

"Jessie, don't play this game," he gritted. "You know damn good and well I can't let you spend the night with him or anyone else now!"

"Why should one dance make you feel so possessive, Lucas?" she murmured.

"You're mine," he rasped softly.

"On what do you base that kind of claim?" she challenged gently.

"On the fact that I made you mine that night in the desert when I laid you down on the sand and made

love to you!'' His hard face was taut and rigid with
the force of his muttered words.

Jessica sensed the power in him, acutely aware of
the manacle-like grip encircling the small bones of her
wrist. ''But that's impossible, Lucas. We just met, remember? By mutual agreement we share no past!''

He must have seen the yawning trap, but he was
too angry to avoid it. ''I won't let you forget that part
of what happened last week!''

''It was your idea,'' she retorted. ''But I'm inclined
to agree with you. It would be impossible to truly forget the whole mess. I can, however, put it behind me
and ignore it. And that's exactly what I intend to do.
Don't feel bad, Lucas. Starting over wouldn't have
worked, anyway.'' She touched the side of his tense
cheek with teasing fingers and felt as if she were deliberately provoking a leopard.

''Why not?'' he asked vengefully.

''You're not my type. Good night, Lucas.'' Snatch-
ing her hand free, Jessica pivoted on one high heel
and made for the small table in the corner where Kirk
still waited.

She only caught scattered glimpses of him for the
rest of the evening. By the time the fabulous midnight
buffet was opened, Jessica thought Lucas must have
given up and gone to bed. Her attention, which had
been divided all evening between trying to enjoy herself with Kirk and an uneasy awareness of Lucas's
presence, began to focus on the manner in which she
intended to end this first night on board ship.

To give the devil his due, Lucas had a point when
he claimed Kirk was hoping for a quick shipboard en-

counter of the sexual kind. But Jessica had been handling a wide variety of men for several years and she knew how to deal with one like Kirk Randall. Although the temptation to bait Lucas had been irresistible, she certainly had no intention of going to bed with Kirk. By the time he had walked her to her stateroom door, he had realized as much and took the sophisticated rebuff with reasonably good grace. As a gesture of appreciation for the fact that he wasn't going to be difficult, Jessica lifted her face for a goodnight kiss.

It was a warm, polished sort of kiss and it did absolutely nothing for her. She was much too polite to show it, however, as they stepped apart.

"Shall I see the purser about adjusting the dining room seating reservations?" Kirk asked tentatively, searching her face for some enthusiasm for the idea.

"Let's not bother," Jessica said quietly. "I'm sure we'll be seeing enough of each other as it is and you don't want everyone to think you're paired off with me."

"Pairing off with you doesn't seem like such a bad idea," he tried coaxingly.

"I'm sure you'd think it was by the end of the cruise," she countered dryly.

"Why?"

"Because I didn't come on board looking for a romantic fling. I'm supposed to be recuperating, remember?"

His mouth turned down wryly at the corner. "Meaning you're not interested in sharing one of these skinny little stateroom beds?"

"I'm afraid not," she said in graceful apology. There was no need to point out that her bed wasn't particularly skinny or uncomfortable. Nor was her stateroom cramped and small. Scanlon had shipped her out first class. As usual.

"Well, I've still got a lot of time to help you change your mind," Kirk said gallantly, but they both knew he would be prowling elsewhere the next day. A cruise lasted for far too short a period of time to allow a man the luxury of wasting time on elaborate courtship. "Good-night, Jessie. I'll see you around, I'm sure."

She watched him walk down the carpeted corridor and then stepped into her room and closed the door.

The sight of the dark male figure standing in the shadows and gazing out the wide stateroom window made her breath catch in her throat. "Lucas! What are you doing here? How did you get inside my room? And what the hell gives you the right in the first place?" As if to lessen the aura of masculine menace in the shadowy room, Jessica stabbed a finger at the light switch as he turned to face her. Furiously she confronted him, not wanting to admit, even to herself, how much his unexpected presence had shaken her.

"Thank you, Jessie," he said simply.

"For what?"

"For not bringing him inside your room."

"It would have served you right if we'd gone to his room instead!" she choked out.

"That wasn't likely," he returned with a rueful grimace. "I checked. His stateroom is on the same deck as mine. Inside and very small. Not even a porthole. Definitely not in the same class as the one Scanlon booked for you." He flicked an amused glance at the luxurious surroundings of her room. "I figured if you were thinking of flinging your independence in my face, you'd insist on doing it with style and in some comfort!"

"That's true," she managed seethingly. "I'm definitely not into 'roughing it.'" She hoped he got the gibe. He did.

"Except when there's no alternative?" Lucas questioned gently.

"A Scanlon employee is trained to cope. With anything!"

"And is, in turn, rewarded well by the company, I can see. What's your home like? Full of French furniture and Oriental rugs?"

"I have an apartment in a Scanlon hotel in downtown L.A. Not that it's any of your business."

"You *live* in a hotel?" He appeared somewhat staggered at the thought.

"Why not? It's a beautiful place and I'm near my work," she pointed out with a dismissing shrug.

"But a hotel! No one lives in a hotel. That's not a home!"

"It is to me and has been for some time. Look, Lucas, I'd appreciate it if you'd get out of here. It's late and I'd like to get some sleep. I signed up for that early morning aerobics dance class."

"You live in a hotel," he was saying, ignoring her request. "Scanlon has the power to whisk you away from an airport in the middle of nowhere after a media event like a plane crash, keep you incognito for three solid days, and then give you two weeks on a luxury cruise. The only person who greets you after you've been missing for five days is a representative of Scanlon. Your pool towel is embroidered with Scanlon's logo and your luggage carries a Scanlon hotel address. Tell me, if we'd had better lighting that night in the desert would I have been able to find a Scanlon tattoo somewhere on your very soft body? Do they own you? It's beginning to sound as if the firm plays the role of family in your life!''

"It does!" she shot back, annoyed.

"And when you marry?" he pursued relentlessly, appearing vastly curious.

Jessica's chin came up aggressively. "If and when I decide to marry," she emphasized carefully, "it will undoubtedly be to someone within the 'family'!"

"You really mean that, don't you?" he breathed.

"Yes!"

"That man who met you at the airport?"

"Lucas, I want you out of here! Now!" she hissed furiously.

He dismissed that, striding forward abruptly to cup her face between rough palms. "Honey, this is incredible and intolerable. You can't make a company like Scanlon into your family. You can't live in a hotel for the rest of your life! Hell, I'll bet they don't even allow you to have pets! You're too soft and womanly and gentle. I've had a chance to learn about the other side of you, don't forget. If you deny that part of your nature, you'll regret it," he told her earnestly.

"You know nothing about me. What you saw of me last week was not a normal or even a very real side of my nature. How many times do I have to tell you that?'' Jessica retorted wearily; then a flash of humor lit her blue-green gaze. ''Besides, I don't want a pet. Too much trouble.''

He saw the warning gleam in her expression and backed down. ''Okay, okay, Jessie, I don't want to send you up in flames again. Believe it or not I waited for you tonight because I wanted to tell you I'm sorry.'' He released her to run a hand through his dark hair. ''I'm sorry,'' he repeated helplessly.

''About what?'' she asked suspiciously.

''About making you afraid of me. About having to do what I did a week ago when I took command after the plane went down. About not realizing until now how alienated you are from the gentler side of your own nature. About trying to enforce a claim on you that you're clearly not ready to accept. About a lot of things, Jessie.''

''That's quite a list. What's all this leading up to, Lucas?''

''Jessie, give me another chance. Let me show you that the part of me you saw in the desert last week isn't all there is to my nature. Honey, let me show you we're right for each other.'' He smiled crookedly. ''I'm quite domesticated, you know. Good company, well-mannered, housebroken, and not inclined to wander.''

''Any obedience training?'' she heard herself ask wryly, responding to the humor in him in spite of herself.

One heavy brow lifted. ''You prefer your men on a leash?''

''With a choke-chain collar!''

"Well, I'm not exactly a lap dog," he hedged carefully, "but unless I'm unduly provoked I can guarantee a certain level of obedience. I *am* anxious to please. Doesn't that count?"

"Oh, Lucas, this is ridiculous. You sound like some dog at the city pound looking for a home!"

"You're the one who seems to need a home," he countered. "Jessie, Jessie, please give yourself a chance to get to know me. Surely you don't have to fear me on board this boat. You said as much, yourself. Let me show you I'm not the man you fled from the day the helicopter picked us up and carried us back to civilization."

"Lucas, I don't…"

"Just give me your word you'll stop avoiding me. Please, sweetheart. If nothing else, at least let me have that much!"

Jessica moved uneasily. "I'm not avoiding you, Lucas," she began, and then halted the blatantly untrue protest before she could perjure herself further. "All right, I suppose I was avoiding you. But if I stop doing that, you're liable to think I want to spend my free time with you, and I don't!"

"I'll take it one step at a time, honey," he promised soothingly. "Think of me as a cute, cuddly, obedient, good-natured pet. When was the last time you owned a pet?"

"When I was six. It was a fish and it never did learn to come when I called it!" she snapped spiritedly.

He grinned. "You won't have that problem with me, I promise."

"Don't give me that spaniel look," she protested with budding laughter. She stepped away from the door and opened it for him. "Goodnight, Lucas. See if you can't scent your way back to your own room. Pretend there's a rabbit waiting there for you!"

He hesitated and then obediently moved toward the door. He paused at the threshold to stare searchingly down at her for a long moment. "I'll go. You give me your word you won't spend tomorrow running away from me again?"

Jessica's eyes chilled. "I'm not running from you, Lucas. I never run from any man!"

For a minute she feared he might call her on the lie, but then he seemed to come to a decision. Bending his head Lucas brushed his mouth against hers in the lightest of kisses and then he was gone.

For a long time Jessica stood leaning back against the door she had closed behind him. She knew she didn't dare release her grip on the knob, because then she would have to confront the unpleasant fact that her fingers were trembling. From fear? From anger? From annoyance?

The answer was that her fingers trembled from excitement. Somehow that seemed far more dangerous to acknowledge than any of the other emotions. It was an excitement she had never experienced with any other man and it made absolutely no sense at all that she should feel it around Lucas Kincaid.

The next morning, dressed in a black leotard and tights, which outlined the slender curves of her figure, Jessica threw herself energetically into following the aerobic dance instructions of a female member of the ship's entertainment staff. The before-breakfast exercise class was filled with women and one masculine, cheerfully gay couple. Among the women, Jessica was quite certain she spotted several of the singles with whom Lucas had danced the night before in the lounge. She couldn't resist sizing them up covertly. Even at this hour, their bodies growing damp with perspiration, most of them appeared quite attractive.

When the class drew to a close, it was the redhead who smiled at Jessica and crossed the deck to speak to her. "I saw you give that interesting man at the bar a whirl last night," she chuckled. "I did, too. My name's Selena Harris, by the way. Waste of time, wasn't it?"

"He, uh, did ask me to dance," Jessica admitted quietly, wiping the sheen of dampness from the back of her neck with a towel.

"Did he step all over your feet and spend the whole time apologizing?" the other woman asked, with a knowing grin.

"Well, he did apologize about a few things." Jessica hid a strange smile.

"I should have realized from the way he was dressed that he wasn't quite what I'd hoped to run into on a cruise. Not exactly the polished, sophisticated type, was he? When he wasn't apologizing, did he talk to you about such exciting topics as the care and feeding of Angel Fish?"

"We did discuss pets at one point during the evening," Jessica agreed dryly.

"Unfair, isn't it? I mean, there's something rather intriguing about the man. A certain appeal in that hard, rugged look. I was hoping he'd turn out to be a dynamic corporate executive,'' Selena sighed regretfully. "I fantasized about him being a ruthless fighter who had surged up the corporate ladder and now desperately needed a mate to help him share life at the top. Of course, when I got a closer look at the clothes he was wearing, I realized he had a way to go to get to the top, but, by then it was too late. I'd already committed myself to a dance.''

A rich, throaty feminine laugh interrupted before Jessica was obliged to answer. She turned to see one of the blondes approaching, a rueful smile in her beautifully made-up eyes. Jessica wondered why anyone would make up her eyes for an early morning exercise class. "Sorry, couldn't help overhearing that last remark. I have a hunch we're talking about the same man. Lucas Kincaid? Personally I was hoping he'd turn out to be a wildly successful lawyer. Recently divorced, of course, and in need of consolation. But a pet shop owner? Listen, friends, I now know more about the dietary habits of hamsters than I ever really wanted to know. Where's the justice in this world when the one man in the lounge who looked like he might be terrific in bed turns out to be the meek, mild owner of a pet shop who's on a cruise for his health!''

Jessica blinked, swallowing her astonishment and the curious wave of intrigue that followed. Were they discussing the same man? Didn't they realize Lucas Kincaid was quite capable of making a woman feel stalked, cornered, and possessed? That if he chose, he could master people or situations with a will that was laced with iron?

No, she realized a second later, these two didn't know what she had learned the hard way. They had no idea of the existence of another side of Lucas's personality.

The knowledge that only she was aware of the secret sent a thrill along her nerve endings, together with a flash of dark humor. Lucas had promised her he was housebroken and reasonably obedient. These women wouldn't have doubted such a promise for an instant. The image of a leopard on a leash flashed through Jessica's mind as she walked back to her cabin for a shower before breakfast. The notion of Lucas Kincaid leashed and under control was deeply challenging.

Five

The enticing mental picture of a dangerous jungle cat on a leash, the end of which was held in her hand, was still flickering in and out of Jessica's head later that morning as she took her seat at breakfast. Lucas and the Howards were already there, sipping coffee and poring over the extensive menu.

"Good morning, everyone," she sang out with a cheerfulness which appeared to take all three of her seatmates by surprise. Of one accord they all glanced up.

"Good morning, Jessie. You look as if you had a restful night," Mrs. Howard ventured hopefully. Jessica felt a pang of remorse. Had she intimidated these nice people by making them witnesses to the undeniable tension between herself and Lucas?

"Must be the sea air and an early morning exercise class," she told Ann Howard with mock gravity as she sat down and picked up the menu. "What's for breakfast?"

"Just about everything you can possibly imagine," Lucas said politely. "Except marinated squid. Mercifully, the chef seems willing to save that for dinner. I'm not sure the three of us could stand to watch you eat it at this hour of the day." His gray gaze moved over her with a veiled expression, taking in the attractive picture she made, invigorated and lively from the aerobics class.

Jessica had changed into a rakish white cotton camp shirt and white pants. Her tawny hair was brushed straight back and caught with a clip at the nape of her neck. She looked and felt carefree and prepared to enjoy her vacation to the fullest. When Lucas's gaze settled questioningly on her face, Jessica returned the glance with a charming smile. "One should always be open to new experiences, Lucas," she admonished in response to his remark about the squid. "As someone once said, one eats what's available." It had been Abby Morgan's comment to the children about the suitability of eating rabbit and Jessica saw at once that he remembered it.

Humor replaced the shuttered, watchful gleam in Lucas's eyes and she could almost see him relaxing as he realized she was going to banter with him. He looked very good to her this morning, she found herself thinking vaguely. Automatically she tried to put the face of the man she knew into the frame her dance-class companions had created. It didn't fit very well. Lucas was wearing a pair of jeans and a white cotton shirt, open at the throat and with the sleeves rolled casually up on his forearms. His hair appeared to have been first tossed by the wind and then combed roughly with his hand and she guessed he'd been for an early morning jog around the upper deck. Some mornings his hair had looked precisely the same way out in the desert when he'd risen early to start a small fire for the brush tea.

There was something infinitely compelling about the conflicting image of a domesticated cat and a sleek wild animal. She had been so certain that Lucas was the latter, yet those other women had been equally sure they had been dancing with a rather dull tabby. Perhaps they were all correct. Perhaps there was more than one side to Lucas, just as he had claimed. What would it be like for a woman to know both sides?

"Is something unfastened that shouldn't be?" Lucas inquired, breaking into her reverie.

"What?" Jessica lowered her lashes, confused. Across the table Bill Howard chuckled.

"You were staring at me and I wondered if I'd forgotten to do up something crucial," Lucas explained helpfully.

"No, no, of course not," Jessica mumbled and concentrated on the menu. "I think I'll start with the papaya and lime. What are you going to have, Ann?"

A discussion of the menu got Jessica through the next few minutes and by the time everyone at the table was digging into various egg dishes the conversation was flowing smoothly.

"I've done a little deep-sea fishing off the coast at Mazatlán," Lucas remarked in regard to a question from Bill. "I think we're due to stop there on the way back from Acapulco. We should make it a point to try to charter a boat for the day we'll be in port. It's quite an adventure.''

Remembering the fishing tackle box that he'd been carrying on the plane, a spark of mischief made Jessica put in easily, ''Isn't your hobby of fishing a bit difficult to justify to all the tropical fish you sell as pets?''

''Fish have a very straightforward sort of philosophy,'' Lucas retorted equably, eyes glinting. ''They'll eat anything smaller than themselves. They would be the first to understand my right to go after what I want.''

''Cold-blooded creatures,'' she murmured.

''Me or the fish?'' he challenged gently. He was practically daring her to call him cold-blooded. If she did, Jessica knew instinctively, he would say or do something to remind her of that night in the desert sand.

''I was speaking of the fish,'' she demurred.

''Umm.'' He nodded wisely. ''Rather like lady hotel executives in that the only thing they fear is something or someone bigger and stronger than they are.''

Jessica's aquamarine gaze narrowed fractionally as she realized Lucas was more than willing to respond to the taunting. ''Surely that's not a totally irrational fear?''

''Not for a fish,'' he admitted readily. ''But it is for a lady executive.''

''Why?''

''Because she has other means of defense besides fleeing.'' He took a huge bite out of a biscuit slathered with honey.

Jessica hesitated, pouring cream into her coffee. "You may be right," she said lightly.

Before Lucas could respond, Ann Howard was interrupting with a comment to the effect that they would be reaching Acapulco in two more days. Jessica had the impression the Howards had silently decided to act as referees at the dining table. "Are you going to attend that lecture on buying Mexican crafts and products, Jessie?" the older woman asked brightly.

"Yes, I think I will. I've heard the horror stories about people who thought they were getting fabulous deals on silver only to find out it was really tin!"

When the foursome broke up after breakfast, Jessica didn't try to evade Lucas as he fell into step beside her. "Where are you headed?" he asked, sliding his fingers firmly through hers.

"The pool, I think. I'm going to direct my energies into building up an appetite for the mid-morning bouillon break!

He grimaced. "Then comes lunch and then afternoon tea with scones and then dinner again. Where will it all end?"

"In a size larger swimsuit if I'm not careful," she laughed.

Lucas grinned, clearly enjoying the pleasure on her face. "No harm in that. You're a little too much on the fashionably thin side as it is."

"You could be right. Perhaps if I were a little bigger and a little stronger I wouldn't have to worry about being swallowed up."

Lucas halted, tugging her to a stop beside him, the humor vanishing immediately from his gaze as he stood looking down at her. "Jessie, you're not really afraid of me, are you?"

Jessica took a deep, considering breath. Afraid of this man who had succeeded in boring some of the most beautiful women on the ship? Afraid of him when she was surrounded by nearly a thousand other people, a large proportion of which were ship's officers? Afraid of a man who looked at her so anxiously?

"No," she declared positively. "Why should I be afraid of an ex-cop? You're no longer in a position to arrest me, are you?"

"Definitely not," he affirmed, relaxing again at the obvious humor in her. "And even if I were, at the moment I'm clearly outside my jurisdiction."

With that a new mood settled on the relationship and the day. Jessica was well aware of it. For the rest of the afternoon she found herself quite content to spend her time with Lucas. They lazed by the pool until lunch, soaking up the sun and talking idly of a variety of things, none of which included their adventure the previous week. The other women in her dancing class had been right, Jessica was forced to admit with an inner smile, Lucas did like to discuss his pet shop business.

The difference was that, unlike the other women, Jessica was astonished to discover that the subject didn't bore her at all. "What about snakes?" she inquired curiously as she lay on her back, the huge white Scanlon towel beneath her, eyes closed behind dark glasses.

"I tried one and I have a feeling I'm going to be stuck with him forever. His main appeal seems to be for small boys. I must have sold that damn snake ten different times during the past six months!''

"Ten times!" she exclaimed.

"I keep having to refund the money when the kid returns it," Lucas sighed.

"Ah, let me guess. Boy buys snake and takes it home. Mom sees snake. Kid returns snake the next day," Jessica outlined wisely.

"Usually within a few hours. Poor Clarence doesn't know whether he's coming or going." Lucas levered himself lazily up on one elbow to sip from his iced tea. "Maybe he'd be good marinated like that squid," he added thoughtfully as he lay back down on his lounger.

"Clarence is the snake?"

"Yeah."

"What does Clarence eat?"

There was silence from the next lounger for a moment. Then Lucas finally said dryly, "Snakes aren't exactly vegetarians, you know."

"Oh, no!" Jessica made a face behind her dark glasses. "Live food? You have to sacrifice cute little white mice?"

"I can usually locate a small kid to feed him for me. Kids seem to have a rather morbid scientific bent. And there's usually any number of them hanging around a pet shop."

"Snakes?"

"Kids," he corrected with a chuckle.

Jessica thought about that, her eyes still closed. "You like kids, don't you? You were terrific with Sharon and Matt." It was the first reference she had made to the five days they had spent in the desert, and she wasn't totally surprised when again there was a pause from the lounger beside her.

Jessica turned her head to glance curiously at Lucas. He was lying on his back, his lean, tanned body stretched out in the sun, and she shifted her gaze rather quickly at the sight of him clad only in sleek swim trunks. The image sent a remembered and unwelcome shiver of desire through her own slender frame. Hastily she tried to bank the glowing spark.

"I like kids," Lucas finally said, slowly.

She remembered the night he'd patiently pointed out the constellations in the desert sky to the children. "Kids and pets," she chuckled wonderingly. "Anyone who likes kids and pets..." She let the sentence trail off, astounded by what she had been about to say.

"Can't be all bad?" he concluded hopefully. "What about you, Jessie? You were pretty good with the youngsters, yourself. I had the feeling they accepted you in the role of surrogate mother during the five days."

"And you as the surrogate father?" she put in wryly.

"Yes," he said steadily. "When you and I, uh, hashed out our differences of opinion, poor Sharon was afraid it was a repeat of the kind of arguments her parents had indulged in, wasn't she?"

"Hashed out our differences of opinion!" Jessica echoed mockingly. "That's a euphemistic phrase if ever I heard one!"

"Well, at least you can laugh about it now," Lucas shot back quietly. "That's a good sign."

"There's nothing like getting back to the real world to put things into proper perspective, is there?" she returned in liquid tones. It was the truth.

Again a pause from Lucas. "You never answered my question."

"About kids? I don't know, Lucas," she replied honestly. "I've never spent much time around them."

"The Scanlon hotel world doesn't cater to children?" he drawled.

"Not particularly. We aim more for the international traveler and the vacationing, two-income couple. We get kids into the hotels, of course, but I rarely encounter them."

"Or pets?"

She laughed. "I'm afraid we don't encourage pets, either."

"Doesn't it seem like a fantasy world sometimes?" he persisted gently.

"Perhaps, but it's a very pleasant fantasy and it's been good to me," she told him firmly. Her tone of voice was meant to warn him off; he backed down at once, letting the subject drop immediately.

The knowledge that Lucas was going out of his way not to antagonize her or push controversial subjects pleased Jessica. He was trying very hard not to offend. She relaxed a little more beneath the hot sun as the ship moved with stately grace toward its destination.

In fact, Jessica told herself as the afternoon came and went, the whole situation was becoming downright amusing. Lucas was acting as if he were walking on eggs around her. He was considerate, attentive, and careful to please, obviously determined to prove himself a charming companion. Charming to her, at least, Jessica clarified silently at one point. What would her aerobic dance companions think about him if they were in her position?

After all, nothing could alter the fact that Lucas wasn't a wealthy and recently divorced businessman or lawyer. A pet shop owner wasn't very likely to be deemed a "good catch" by some women. But Jessica knew that she, personally, had never been so deeply aware of, or intrigued by, a man in her life. Now that she seemed to have him and the situation under control, she could free her mind to examine the curious electricity that sparked between them.

That night she danced once more in Lucas's arms after dinner, amused at the benevolent smiles the Howards had showered on them during the meal. It was easy to give herself to the masculine grace of his body on the dance floor, perhaps a little too easy. Lucas held her close, folding her into the heat of his body. Later they made their way through the small, glittering casino on a lower deck. Lucas teased her into throwing several coins into a gleaming slot machine and then they wound up the evening with a walk around the moonlit deck.

Jessica was still asking herself how she would deal with him at the end of the evening as they approached her stateroom door. He silently took the key from her hand, unlocked the door and stood aside.

As he shut out the corridor behind them, she turned, pivoting smoothly around to find herself in his arms. Jessica felt the possessive but still-lashed strength in his arms as they circled her, heard her name whispered

in a husky, masculine plea, and then all thought of
firmly dismissing him faded from her mind as his
mouth found hers. There was no harm in letting him
kiss her, she thought wildly. After all, there had been
no harm in him all day.

Whatever she had been subconsciously expecting
from his embrace, however, one thing was immediately clear. Lucas was still bent on practicing restraint
in every aspect of the relationship. For some obscure
reason, that annoyed her. Jessica realized belatedly
that she wanted him to want her.

Deliberately she leaned against him, her hands sliding around his neck as she let herself respond to the
pull of the undeniable attraction they shared. His
mouth seemed to harden with heightened desire,
slowly increasing its demands. Jessica knew a part of
her reveled in the reaction she was provoking. Here it
was safe to indulge some of the passion that was flooding through her. Surrounded by the luxury and built-
in protection of her sophisticated lifestyle, Jessica began to examine the tantalizing idea that had crept in-
sidiously into her mind during the day. What would it
be like to have an affair with Lucas Kincaid?

An affair with Lucas Kincaid. The temptation began
to flicker in her head like an internal, beckoning fire.
Surely such an idea should have been the last thing
on her mind, given past circumstances. Or had the seed
been planted out there on the desert, waiting for safe,
fertile soil to grow?

"Jessie, Jessie," he groaned, prying his mouth from
hers. "You're going to drive me crazy tonight and I've
already spent so many sleepless nights recently!"

Confused by her own reactions and the wild notion of an affair, Jessica pulled slightly away from him, her hands fluttering with unconscious sensuality down his neck to his shoulders. "Why am I going to drive you crazy?" she whispered as his palms moved across the expanse of her back, which was bared by the small, black evening dress she had worn that evening. There had been something delightfully unexpected and mildly shocking about wearing black in the warmth of a balmy summer night. But the gown was cut with the sparseness of a sundress and it had made a dashing statement at dinner and later on the dance floor.

"Because you're going to send me away tonight, aren't you?" he answered knowingly. There was a note of resignation underlying his words. His eyes roved her face, clearly expecting to find no hope.

"Lucas," Jessica heard herself say with surprising honesty, "I'm confused. Everything is happening too quickly. This morning I never expected to find myself in this position tonight!"

"I know. Even though I'm going to lie in my bed staring at the bulkhead until dawn, I'm not complaining." His hard mouth crooked gently. "Much," he amended dryly. "I'm just grateful we've finally made a start. Goodnight, Jessie. Sleep well."

With a last, lingering caress, Lucas released her and let himself out the door, leaving Jessica staring in bemused silence at the solid sheet of painted metal.

What did she want from Lucas Kincaid? Why was she beginning to fantasize about something as dangerous as an affair with the man? Not very long ago she had told herself she never wanted to see him again!

Slowly she undressed and crawled into bed, trying to analyze her emotions. What was she trying to prove? That here in her world she could deal with a man like Lucas? That she could subtly master him the way he had once mastered her?

Restlessly she raised herself to a kneeling position on the bed, turning to gaze out at the moonlit sea beyond her stateroom window. That must be it. A part of her wanted to prove something, now that it seemed safe to do so. She wanted to know she could go to bed with the man without feeling as if she'd surrendered. She wanted to put their relationship on a sophisticated, modern, thoroughly manageable level, a level she could control beyond any question.

Jessica blinked in the darkness as the full realization hit her. There were two things she wanted now from Lucas Kincaid. She wanted to wipe out the memory of how it had been between them that night in the desert and she wanted to prove to herself that in the real world she could handle Lucas Kincaid.

Her motives clear to herself at last, Jessica had no trouble at all going straight to sleep.

The next day was spent with Lucas in a round of pleasant shipboard activities. The undemanding nature of cruise life allowed plenty of time for the subtle, teasing sensuality that flickered between Lucas and Jessica. At times she thought her delicate feminine provocation confused him. At other times he seemed grateful for it, as if he were determined not to question the reason behind her willingness to dance the intricate steps which led toward a sophisticated, modern affair.

He was too good a fisherman to question his luck, Jessica thought with wry humor.

There were occasions during the day when she would find him watching her with a strangely hooded expression that would clear the instant he realized she noticed it. The expression was a little too intent, too searching, and it disturbed her, but she told herself it was a manifestation of his desire to play the game as cautiously as possible. His caution pleased her. It was as if they had changed roles and he was now the one who must wait to be chosen. That last thought occurred to her late in the afternoon as they lay once again beside the pool, recovering from tea and scones.

"What's so amusing?" Lucas suddenly demanded.

"Nothing really, I'm just relaxing," she lied. There was no way she could tell him she'd been imagining him in such a role reversal!

"Umm." He seemed skeptical and she slid a glance across at him from behind the safety of the sunglasses. "I thought you might be smiling back at one of those two guys sitting across the pool in deck chairs," he admitted.

Automatically Jessica glanced up. Two very attractive men, wearing incredibly tiny designer swim trunks, sat gazing toward Lucas and herself from behind dark glasses. Jessica's smile widened gleefully. "I'm afraid it's you they're watching, not me," she chuckled, shutting her eyes again. "I met them both in my aerobic class. Very charming and very gay."

"What?" He sounded mildly startled and then he grinned ruefully. "Oh, I see." He hesitated and then asked devilishly, "Jealous?"

Jessica pitched an ice cube from her soft drink onto his bare, warm stomach. Lucas's yelp was quite satisfying. He jackknifed erect, grabbing for her in the same motion. Before she quite realized what had happened, he had picked her up and surged to his feet, intent on tossing her into the pool.

"Lucas!" A physical shock went through her as his strong arms closed around her, rendering her helpless. Instantly the laughter died in her eyes and she went rigid in his arms. He was only teasing her, she reminded herself frantically, and she could control him. "Put me down. And not in the water!" she ordered with a fierceness unwarranted by the situation.

He halted immediately, the humor fading from his iron-colored eyes as he looked down at her in his arms and realized she meant business. "You deserve this, Jessie," he tried lightly, but he didn't open his arms and let her fall. She knew in that moment that he didn't quite dare, and a combination of relief and exhilaration soared through her. The tension seeped out of her as Jessica looked up into his face.

"Put me back on the lounger, Lucas. I have no intention of going back into the water just yet." It was a test and they both knew it. The small clash of wills would be fateful, but she knew with rising certainty that she would win it.

Without a word he swung around and set her gently back on the lounger, his face taut and concerned. She had given him a scare, Jessica thought coolly. Her mouth curved in satisfaction and relief. "Good boy," she drawled impudently, resisting the urge to reach out and pat him on the head like a puppy.

Without taking his eyes off her face, Lucas sank down on the pool chair next to hers, leaning forward with his elbows resting on his knees, his large hands clasped together. She had the feeling he had entwined his fingers in an effort to keep himself from taking hold of her. Perhaps by the throat. For a taut moment, silence reigned between them; then Lucas relaxed sufficiently to smile wryly and tug at an imaginary collar around his neck.

"I think I just felt the choke-chain," he growled.

Jessica's smile widened and then she was grinning at him. "You can't get away with some of the tactics you used a week ago. Not here in the real world," she said lightly.

He sighed and leaned back in the chair. "Jessie, I was only teasing."

"I know."

"And you were only testing?" he quipped.

"Yes." Settling herself more comfortably, Jessica decided to change the subject. "Tell me, did you see any of the others after we were rescued?"

"Sharon and Matt left the airport with their parents. I didn't see them again. I'm afraid the kids read a little too much into the fact that both parents came to meet them, though," he added sadly.

"You mean they started hoping that somehow Mommy and Daddy would forgive each other?" Jessica sympathized.

"It looked that way to me. I'm afraid they'll all have to go through the break again. Do you remember how Sharon was afraid that our argument was analogous to the ones her parents apparently had had?"

"I remember. She was afraid I would make you so angry that you'd leave us all on our own out there," Jessica murmured wryly.

"But you assured her I wouldn't abandon any of you because of an argument." He turned his head to trap her gaze. "It's the truth, Jessie. I wouldn't walk out on you because of an argument."

"Well, it was a pretty safe bet you weren't the type to leave all of us alone in the desert and go off in search of personal rescue!" she retorted, deliberately misunderstanding him.

"Jessie, I'm talking about us. You and me. You can't drive me away. Do you understand what I'm saying?"

"You're saying you're the persistent type," she mocked, refusing to let him turn the conversation in such a personal direction. She wasn't ready for it. "What about the others? Did you see them?"

He hesitated and then apparently gave up his attempt to discuss their relationship. "I talked to Dave for a few minutes before he left with his father. Told him to keep in touch. He's stationed at Camp Pendleton near San Diego, so I'll probably see him again one of these days."

"He was nice. I liked him. He idolized you."

Lucas ignored that. "Abby and Mabel claim they're going to write a cookbook on a hundred and one ways to cook rabbit."

"I'll be sure to get an autographed copy," Jessica chuckled. "Even though I don't ever intend to eat rabbit again in my lifetime! What about Gary, the co-pilot?"

"Desolate at not seeing you before you cut out on us," Lucas told her bluntly.

"What do you mean?"

"The poor guy had a crush on you. You must have been aware of it. Perfectly logical, of course. You were the one he saw bending over him every time he woke up in the middle of the night with a splitting head-ache!"

"You're kidding!" Jessica was genuinely startled. "A crush? On me?"

"He'll get over it," Lucas decided laconically.

Jessica shook her head once in disbelief. She had been aware of no other man in that sense except Lucas.

"I would probably have been jealous as hell if I hadn't realized you were treating him strictly as a nurse treats a patient!"

"Oh, I doubt that he would have represented any sort of real threat to you, even if he hadn't been ill!" Jessica said without thinking. There was a tinge of bitterness in her words that Lucas heard immediately. "You were indisputably in charge!"

"Until I'm sure of you, any other man represents a threat," he admitted calmly.

"Fortunately here in civilization there's not much you can do about potential *threats,* is there?" she asked caustically. He just looked at her for a long moment, saying nothing, and then he signaled the steward for another iced tea.

The strange tension that had developed during their conversation had not disappeared when Jessica joined her tablemates again that evening for dinner. It was a subtle thing and she wasn't even sure the Howards

were aware of it. But Lucas was, Jessica knew. He
was aware of it and fearful of it, afraid that she would
use it as an excuse to give him the cold shoulder.
Realizing that, she took great pleasure in doing just
the opposite. It was a delicious challenge, this business
of keeping Lucas Kincaid hanging on tenterhooks, she
decided as she ignored the wary glances of the others
and eagerly consumed a plate of sashimi. The selection
of raw fish served Japanese style had never tasted better. The ship's chef was excellent. After two glasses
of the elegant German Riesling wine she had chosen
for the table, the challenge of Lucas became more and
more irresistible.

"Would you like to go see the cabaret act?" he
inquired politely as they left the dining room an hour
later. His hand slid possessively under her arm as she
walked beside him.

"Yes, I would," Jessica said smiling. "And then
perhaps some dancing?"

He nodded quickly, accepting her wishes unhesitat-
ingly. The floor show was a well-staged production,
which included comedy and magic as well as some
good song-and-dance numbers. By the time the per-
formance had ended, Jessica had made up her mind.
When Lucas took her into his arms later on the dance
floor, she went with a willingness that seemed to surprise him. Once again, however, he didn't ask any
questions, apparently content to take whatever was offered.

She could feel the sensual tension radiating from
his body as the night deepened around them and knew
that her own body was vibrating in response. Her de-

cision had been made and now she allowed her excitement full scope. It thrilled her to know that he was as aware of the gathering storm as she, but still trying desperately to keep himself under control. Was he so afraid she would turn away again tonight? Jessica thought wonderingly.

"Jessie?" he rasped heavily as he led her out of the lounge and into the soft, sea-scented night on the open deck. She said nothing, not trusting herself to speak, but nestled into the hard warmth of his shoulder. Wordlessly he held her, his strong hands working against her skin with violently repressed desire. Feeling it, she moved against him, her fingertips sliding up along the sleeve of his corduroy jacket. He groaned and held her lower body against his hardening thighs, letting her know the full extent of his need.

"Oh, Lucas," she finally whispered as a shiver of anticipation and flaring heat raced through her. "Lucas, do you want me?"

"More than anything else on this earth," he breathed shakily and buried his lips in the curve of her neck. "I've never wanted any woman the way I want you. Please, darling…!"

Tonight he must beg for her. He could not simply lead her off into the wilderness and lay her down beneath the stars. Tonight the power to bestow herself rested solely in her own hands. Jessica lifted her face and the moonlight reflected softly in her aqua eyes, darkening them with ancient mystery and the glint of feminine desire. Tonight the power was hers and she could use it to obliterate the memory of how it had been between herself and Lucas a week ago. Tonight she could even the relationship; put it on a proper, modern level. Tonight she would prove to herself and to him that she could handle Lucas Kincaid.

"If I go with you," she began very softly, "it will be because I wish it."

"Yes." He didn't argue with her right to make the decision. She felt the hardness of his body and knew that it was aching for the release of a woman, but he would not argue with her right. Lucas was back in civilization now. He had no option but to play by the rules of society. "Jessie, please come to me. Let me make love to you tonight. Don't turn me away again at your door, sweetheart, I need you so badly!"

She closed her eyes and took a deep breath and then she relaxed against his tough frame. "Yes, Lucas."

She felt the shudder which went through him and then he gently lifted her chin for the softest of kisses. Very carefully, as if she were made of crystal and he was terrified of dropping her on the hard deck, Lucas wrapped her close to his side and started toward the entrance nearest to her stateroom.

Six

The red-carpeted corridor which led to Jessica's state-room was empty at this hour. Everyone else on board was busy enjoying the extensive nightlife available. In silence Lucas walked her down the hall, reached word-lessly for her key, and opened the door. As she stepped inside her room, a sense of the inevitability of the moment assailed her, reminding her forcibly of her emotions that night under the desert sky.

The sensation alarmed her briefly. This wasn't how she wanted to feel! This time was to be different. This time everything would be on her terms. Jessica turned to confront Lucas as he shut the door behind them.

He stood still for a moment, the hard planes of his face visible in the glow of the room's soft light. The iron-colored eyes were shadowed and deep with de-sire. But she saw that the tension in him was more than sexual and knew he was wary. The knowledge eased the nervous uncertainty which had sprung alive in the pit of her stomach and Jessica's mouth lifted into a gentle, inviting curve. She was still in control of this moment and this man. That was the only thing that mattered.

"Jessie!" He saw the smile and stepped forward abruptly, enclosing her in his arms for long, silent seconds. They stood together, unmoving, savoring the heat of passion that was building in their bodies, and then Lucas lifted his hands to the smooth knot of her tawny hair. Slowly, reverently, he began to undo the thick mass.

"Sweetheart," he grated huskily, "you won't regret this. I'll show you everything's right between us."

"Will you, Lucas?" she breathed in soft, liquid accents. A thrill of desire rippled along her nerves as the last of her hair came down and he raked his strong hands through the tendrils.

"Yes!" The word was a groan of virile promise. Jessica felt the faint trembling in his fingers as he sensuously began to massage the delicate nape of her neck.

Slowly, in response to the spiraling anticipation uncoiling in her body, Jessica lifted her hands to Lucas's shoulders, her peach-tinted nails sinking luxuriously, tantalizingly into the roughness of his corduroy jacket. Her head arched backward as his fingers traced increasingly sensual designs on the incredibly sensitive area just above her shoulders.

"Jessie, I want you so badly. Please, please, don't ever again be frightened of me!"

"I'm not frightened of you, Lucas. Why should I

be?'' she dared very softly, her lips parting in a summons as old as time.

"Maybe I've got it all backward," he growled thickly as he lowered his head. "Maybe I'm the one who's scared. Of you."

"Yes," she got out huskily and then his mouth was on hers, probing, persuading, pleading. Jessica felt her entire being come shimmeringly awake to the promise of that kiss. Her nails dug more deeply into the fabric of his jacket and her mouth blossomed like a flower to invite the exquisite sting of his hovering tongue.

Lucas groaned as he surged into the dark velvet behind her lips and the strong fingers at the nape of her neck displayed an amazing sensitivity as they slid inside the low neckline of her dress. Jessica's skin seemed to tingle everywhere his hands touched her. Of her own accord she crowded closer into the furnace of his body.

The hard muscles of his taut thighs seemed to cradle her softness as Lucas found the fastening of her dress and slowly undid it. Jessica shivered as his fingers slipped inside the material and gently stroked the skin of her back. The bodice of the gown fell to her waist as she twisted urgently against him, revealing the soft swell of her unconfined breasts.

"God, Jessie!"

The thick desire in his hoarsely uttered words made her slide her hands inside the opening of his jacket, where she found the buttons of his white shirt. Lucas buried his face in the cascading fall of her hair as she exposed his hair-roughened chest to her touch. When they both stood naked from the waist up, he lifted his head to gaze down at her in wonder and still-controlled need.

Slowly he moved his hands from the base of her spine, around her waist, and up her rib cage to the point just beneath the curving weight of her breasts. The iron-colored eyes were dark pools of passion as, his gaze never leaving hers, Lucas carefully rasped his palms across the tautness of her budding nipples.

"Lucas!" She stared up at him from beneath the heavy veil of her lashes, suddenly unable to break the bonds of the iron in his eyes. There was something unbelievably seductive about the way he held her gaze as he explored the delicate tips of her breasts. Jessica knew she could have stepped back at any time, but all she wanted to do was move closer and closer to his touch.

"You're so perfect for me," he whispered, bending his head once more to find her mouth. Instead of sweeping back inside, however, he used the tip of his tongue to outline the shape of her parted lips, until she was moaning far back in the depths of her throat.

Then he swooped and picked her up in his arms, carrying her the short distance to the stateroom bed. There he set her down, still treating her as if he were handling the finest glass. Jessica lay looking up at him, hungry for the look in his eyes which told her of his desire. It fed something in her, something she told herself was a sophisticated, modern form of passion, something totally unlike what she had experienced in the desert.

Lucas stood towering above her in the soft light, drinking in the sight of her sprawled sensuously on the bed, and then his hands went to the buckle of his slacks. Jessica's hooded gaze swept over his blatantly aroused maleness as Lucas stepped out of the remainder of his clothing. Her body trembled in response.

"I could still stop this if I wished," she found herself saying with an unexpected urgency. It was as if she must convince herself as well as him about the truth of the statement.

The words had all the devastating effect she could have wished, and yet Jessica was shocked at the contrition she felt as the color surged up under Lucas's skin. His whole body stiffened and the look in his gray gaze was enough to bring tears to her eyes.

"Jessie, no!" he grated, not moving.

Impulsively, knowing a desperate urge to banish the stunned expression in that hard face, Jessica put out her hand to him and lay back against the pillow. "Come to me, Lucas. I'm not going to send you away. Not tonight."

With a muffled groan he was beside her in a heavy rush, gathering her into his arms with fierce desperation. His lips found the curve of her shoulder and he began dropping quick, stinging little kisses along it up to the pulsepoint at the base of her throat. "Jessie, I would have gone out of my mind if you'd sent me away tonight."

It was the admission she wanted, wasn't it? So why did she bite her lip in a wave of remorse and tenderly stroke his smoothly muscled shoulders? Forget it, Jessica told herself quickly, you have what you want. Everything will be equal this time. Stop worrying about it and take what you need from him now.

Lucas left her throat, moving his mouth down to the swell of her breast, his hands going ahead to slide off the rest of her clothing until she lay naked beside him. When his mouth fastened deliberately on one taut nipple, Jessica moaned again and her legs shifted with languid desire.

As if in response, his hard thigh moved against her softer ones, urging them apart and opening her to his touch more completely. She felt the nip of his teeth on the aroused nipple now as he flattened his hand on her stomach and slowly began tracing circles of tightening ecstasy on her skin. They were not delicate, teasing circles; rather the rough palm of his hand moved with strong, possessive motions, asking a response from her that was answered with an arching tension in her lower body.

"Honey, you're all on fire," he muttered in tones of almost violent satisfaction. "You want me. Please say it!" he pleaded.

"I want you, Lucas." It was the truth and Jessica no longer told herself she had to deny it. Her hips lifted again against the firm touch of his hand and the silkiness of her inner thighs was teased by the roughness of the hard leg inserted between them. It was a heady combination of sensations that washed through her and they were all underlined by the subdued, but ever-present motion of the huge ship. The background throb of its engines seemed to echo the racing pulse that pounded through her veins.

"Jessie, you're the only woman in the world for me now," Lucas confessed raggedly. His stroking hand moved lower, searching out the heated center of her passion until he found his goal.

"Oh, Lucas!" At the intimate touch, Jessica cried out in a voice choked with unbelievable wonder and desire. Her mind cleared of all but the immediate sensations and the immediate knowledge of his presence. Nothing else mattered in this moment. She began to explore the contours of the hard, lean body she remembered so well, her nails circling delicately one moment, kneading deeply into his flesh the next. He gasped aloud at her touch, whispering words of encouragement that made her increasingly eager.

When she cried out once more and began to pull him closer, he suddenly drew back, however.

"Lucas?" she murmured, not understanding as he rolled onto his back. Then she saw the undiminished fire in his eyes and smiled, knowing now what he was doing. He was accepting her right to take the lead tonight, right down to the final ending. With a tight exclamation of passion, Jessica sprawled in sensual abandon across the enticing strength in him, her hair sweeping briefly across his shoulders as she lowered herself to his body.

"Jessie, you're a witch. My desert witch," he muttered, threading his hands through her hair and then sliding them down to her waist. "Make love to me, witch. I need your magic!"

She obeyed with joyous certainty, settling herself so that his body filled hers. He sucked in his breath, his fingers tightening at her hips as she brought them together with taunting, exquisite slowness. She knew he longed to complete the union in a single, thrusting movement, but Jessica took heightened pleasure in forcing a slow, mocking, intimate love-play. Lucas's body was trembling and rigid with the torture to which she was putting him, but he made no move to alter her provocative approach.

Then, when her own need overcame the urge to tantalize, Jessica sighed and succumbed to it. She could feel the shuddering groan deep in his chest as she collapsed fully against him and Lucas's arms came around her with such strength that she wondered how he had tolerated the earlier teasing. But the fleeting thought was pushed aside as he began to move under her, pulling her into the rhythm that found its echo in that of the ship that surrounded them. In tune with the sea, their bodies merged, surging together and then drawing slightly apart. It was the primitive motion of the waves that guided the pattern of their lovemaking and it was as undeniable as the sea itself.

"Jessie, my own!"

She heard her name on his lips, knew the depths of his desire, and it fed her own, stoking it to ever higher levels. The tempo of their union increased, forming now a counterpoint to the waves that rocked them so gently. The strong, muscular hips beneath her lifted with gathering force and Jessica felt Lucas's fingers dig deeply into the resilient curve of her buttocks.

Together they gave themselves up to the moment with an elemental abandon that seemed right. Jessica ceased thinking of the past or the future, throwing herself completely into the reality of the here and now. The man in whose arms she lay was the only being in the universe who counted.

When Lucas felt the small, rippling convulsion that suddenly swept over Jessica, heard his name on her lips, he tensed for one last surge of power and then followed her into the heart of the swirling storm that captured them both completely.

Down, down they tumbled, locked in each other's arms, onto the safety of the seabed. The warm water seemed to cover them both, insulating them for a time and then withdrawing its protective cloak, leaving Lucas and Jessica washed ashore.

It was several long, languorous moments before Lucas broke the filmy silence, shifting slightly to pull her gently closer as he spoke. "What are you thinking about, sweetheart?" He nibbled lazily at her earlobe, which happened to be within reach of his strong, white teeth.

"I'm wondering why you brought me back to my own stateroom instead of taking me down to yours," Jessica murmured lightly. It wasn't quite the truth, but it would serve to set a safe, easy note to the conversation. Some returning sense of caution warned her that that would be best.

"I told you the other night I'm not traveling first class," he chuckled. "And you seem to be very much a first-class sort of woman."

"So we came to my place instead of yours?" she teased, trailing her fingertips through the curling hair on his chest and playing delicately with his flat brown nipples. A sudden thought crossed her mind and she frowned. "Lucas, this trip must have cost you a fortune!"

"About a million parakeets and God knows how

many hamsters,'' he agreed, his mouth crooking humorously. ''But you're worth it.''

''Thanks!'' she giggled.

The laughter faded from his eyes as he gazed down into her upturned face. ''Jessie, are you happy here with me tonight?''

She smiled. ''Yes, Lucas. I'm happy.''

He sighed heavily and his lashes closed briefly in evident relief. ''You've really put me through some hoops during the past few days. Ever since you left me to face that damn crowd of newspaper reporters at the airport after we were rescued!''

''Ah, but you were the hero of the episode. It was your duty to handle the publicity afterward,'' she retorted deliberately.

''I had the impression you weren't terribly impressed with me in the role of hero!'' he complained good-naturedly, nuzzling the soft area behind the ear he had been nibbling.

Jessica lifted one brow as she considered that. ''I'd rather not talk about it, Lucas,'' she finally declared firmly.

''Okay. What would you like to talk about?''

''The midnight buffet?'' she suggested teasingly.

''My God, woman! You just ate a few hours ago!''

''I want you to get your money's worth out of this cruise,'' she chuckled. ''That means eating everything in sight.''

''I think I'm going to need a little more exercise before I can stomach the thought of watching you gobble down raw oysters or stuffed octopus at midnight,'' he told her reflectively.

"Are they serving stuffed octopus at the midnight buffet?" she demanded ingenuously. "How exciting!"

"When was the last time you had some good, plain food?" he growled, his hands beginning to move enticingly on her arm.

"Several days ago, as a matter of fact. I lived off roasted rabbit for quite some time. Remember?" she shot back dryly.

"Ouch. I'd forgotten." He shrugged. "Well, that doesn't count. I'm talking about a good meat loaf and a baked potato."

She laughed. "I never eat meat loaf when I can get lobster."

"And working for Scanlon assures you the choice, right?" he concluded bluntly, pulling his head away to eye her curiously.

Jessica nodded. It was the truth. "Scanlon takes good care of me."

Lucas shook his head admonishingly. "*I'll* take good care of you," he corrected a little roughly and drew her back into his arms with a forcefulness Jessica told herself she should protest but couldn't. Not just then.

Jessica awoke the next morning with the feeling that something had been radically altered in her shipboard world. The heavy weight of a man's arm across her breasts was part of the change and she gingerly slid out from under it, turning on her side to search the sleeping face of the man next to her. In the new light filtering through the stateroom curtain, Lucas had the air of a relaxed and contented predator. The thought made Jessica uneasy and she reminded herself that he was no longer any such thing. There was no menace now in Lucas Kincaid. Last night she had proven that here in the real world she could more than hold her own. A strange smile tilted the edge of her mouth. She could make him jump through hoops! Hadn't he admitted as much?

"A smile like that on a woman's face first thing in the morning is enough to make any sane man refuse to face the remainder of the day!" Lucas grumbled.

"Makes you nervous?" she hazarded brightly, realizing he was studying her through his dark lashes.

"Very."

"Lucas, does something about the ship feel different?" she asked, glancing around as she realized that escaping the confinement of his arm hadn't altered her sense of change.

"We're in port," he yawned. "They've shut down the engines."

"Oh!" Kneeling excitedly, Jessica pulled back the window curtain. "We're anchored in the bay. I can see Acapulco. Come on, let's get going. I have a thousand things to look for in the shops!"

Lucas glanced idly at the watch he still wore. "They won't start ferrying people ashore for another couple of hours. There's no rush, honey."

But he gave in to her excitement and sense of anticipation with indulgent grace and Jessica made certain they were both among the first group of passengers conveyed ashore in the small lifeboat used for that purpose.

Gleaming high-rise hotels lined the shore of Aca-

pulco, concealing in their shadows the far poorer
dwellings and shops of the people who lived in the
Mexican Riviera city. They hadn't been ashore more
than a few minutes when Jessica was eagerly accosted
by a street vendor selling rings. She smiled aloofly and
shook her head, having taken to heart the lecture on
buying Mexican jewelry that had been given to the
ship's passengers. But the man, undaunted, continued
to entreat her to look at his wares. He spoke only a
few words of English and Jessica knew only a similar
number of Spanish phrases. It was Lucas who handled
the situation with a rapid spate of Spanish, which surprised her.

"I didn't know you spoke the language," she observed interestedly as the vendor faded into the crowd,
searching out another likely tourist.

"I've spent a lot of vacation time fishing down
here," he explained easily.

"You know your way around Acapulco?" she demanded, eyes lighting.

"Reasonably well. Why?" He slid a half-amused,
half-suspicious glance at her intrigued features.

"Then you must know where all the best shops
are!"

"I spent my vacation time fishing, not shopping!"
he protested with a grin. But nevertheless, he took her
hand and hailed a taxi. Within a few hair-raising moments, they were deposited in an old section of the
city and Jessica was enthralled with the collection of
chic boutiques mixed in with less sophisticated but just
as appealing shops.

"Jessie," he said quite seriously as she started into

the nearest boutique. "Some of this part of town is pretty rough. Don't go wandering off, okay?"

She glanced around, one sandaled foot already on the first step leading to the open door. "It looks all right to me." Her brightly patterned cotton wrap dress fluttered around her knees, caught by a small breeze.

"Just take my word for it, honey," he advised, following her into the shop.

Jessica frowned at the tone of command that had surfaced momentarily in his voice. A leopard didn't change its spots overnight, she reminded herself, as she began searching through a pile of beautifully printed cotton fabrics.

But maybe this particular leopard hadn't fully realized that his spots had been changed for him!

Jessica spent the next hour wandering happily through the shops, Lucas trailing faithfully in her wake. It was drawing near lunchtime and she was carrying several packages, when she paused in front of a leathercraft store window. The shop was part of a rambling collection of such places filling every corner of a large, open-air building.

"Going to look at hand-tooled bags?" Lucas asked, seeing her fascination with an item in the window.

"What do you think of that purse?" she demanded earnestly, pointing out an elaborately carved, heavy leather bag.

"I think it looks like something you'd only wear on vacation in Mexico!" he chuckled. "Look, take your time. I'm going to check out that silver display over there. Yell if you need me," he added casually and wandered across the old terraced floor to where another vendor had set up a glittering array of polished silver items.

Jessica nodded at his back, smiling as she realized that he was finally leaving her on her own for a while. Not that there could be any danger in this particular building, with its crowds of tourists and hordes of shops. She took another look at the leather bag, her mouth turning downward doubtfully. Perhaps Lucas was right. It might be the sort of thing which looked terrific on location but would be a totally useless addition to her wardrobe back home. Abandoning the purse with a sigh of mild regret, she went on to the next shop in the open-air building.

Twenty minutes later she had come to the end of the wide hall and was about to start working her way up the opposite side of the building when she decided to glance out into the alley behind the market. She was delighted to find that several vendors had set up displays just beyond the door of the large building. A quick glance back down the hall of indoor displays did not reveal Lucas, so Jessica shrugged dismissingly and stepped out into the alley. She would just take a quick look outside and then start back toward where she had left Lucas.

It wasn't long before she realized that one intriguing alley was going to lead to another. Jessica lost track of time as she moved among the collections of pottery, crafts, and the inevitable silver, real and fake, which were set out on brightly colored cloths on the ground. Everywhere enthusiastic vendors praised their wares and her intelligence for stopping to examine them. At least, it sounded like praise to her untutored ears.

She had just declined an interestingly designed hammock, which she knew she'd never be able to hang in her hotel apartment, and had decided to go back into the main building when one last narrow alley caught her attention. She would take a quick look at the tiny shop housed at the opposite end and then she would go find Lucas. She was getting hungry.

Jessica hadn't gone more than a few steps into the warm, shadowy interior of the alley when her senses warned her she'd made a serious mistake. Uneasily, she turned but saw no one behind her. Nevertheless, the impression of being followed persisted. The shop wasn't that important, she decided quickly. She would skip it and return to the main building.

Her sandaled feet carried her quickly back the way she had come, but not quickly enough. A figure in a wide-brimmed hat and a colorful serape stepped into her path, blocking the only exit. Eyes that glittered with malice and a cold smile of evil anticipation flashed from under the hat.

"The señorita is lost?" the man inquired boldly with a totally false solicitousness as he glided forward. The accent was horrible, but Jessica understood every word.

"The señorita is *not* lost," she stated firmly, lifting her chin and walking toward the alley entrance with a self-confidence she was far from feeling. One had to be firm and unafraid in front of a man like this. Lucas had been right this time, though. She shouldn't have ventured so far from the safety of her fellow tourists. Well, she would just have to bluff her way out of the mess and then discreetly not mention anything about it to Lucas!

"I will help the señorita find her way," the man told her, far too smoothly, eyes gleaming as he took in the sight of her packages and the purse that dangled from her shoulder. "But there is a price, you understand."

"I don't need your help," she bit out, aware that the distance between herself and the man was narrowing rapidly. So far he showed no sign of retreating. "Kindly get out of my way," she ordered briskly. Her pulse was beginning to pound with what could only be described as fear. The knowledge thoroughly annoyed her.

"There is a price for that, too, señorita," the man drawled, and quite suddenly the dappled sunlight was glinting off a knife in his hand.

Jessica halted. She wasn't prepared to try walking full tilt into a knife blade. Her heart was racing now as the adrenaline surged into her bloodstream. She would have to try screaming, she told herself. Perhaps if she threw her packages at the man and screamed loudly there would be an opportunity to escape in the confusion.

"The price for leaving this alley is your purse," the man told her coolly. He jerked the tip of the knife upward threateningly. The false smile was gone now, leaving only the hard, shadowed eyes. "Give me the purse, señorita!"

It was going to be now or never. Jessica took a tight grip on her fear and gathered herself to hurl the packages in the general direction of her accoster. The scream wouldn't take much preparation; it would come out quite naturally!

For a split-second Jessica and the man formed a frozen tableau as they confronted each other in the old alley, each waiting for the reaction of the other. And then a third figure stepped into the stark scene.

"Lucas!" Jessica's widening eyes and accompanying exclamation of relief were enough to convince her would-be assailant that there was another factor with which to contend. He spun around and saw Lucas standing, feet braced slightly apart, at the alley entrance.

In that moment Jessica knew that her jungle cat was more than capable of matching the thief when it came to sheer menace. There was a cold, dangerous aura radiating from Lucas Kincaid. The iron in his eyes had never been more evident and the assured strength in his stance spoke volumes to the man who had tried to rob Jessica. Instinctively he seemed to react to the dominance in the stranger, eyes narrowing as he backed away a pace or two.

Lucas spoke, his voice as dark and arrogantly threatening as his stance; then his hand moved in the shadows and Jessica realized with a shock that he also carried a knife. Stunned, she could only stare, listening to the sharp slice of his language as he gave commands to the other man. She didn't understand a word of the Spanish, but the effect on her assailant was immediate and electric.

Without a backward glance at Jessica, the man edged toward the front of the alley. Smoothly, slowly, Lucas stood aside and allowed him to pass, his eyes never leaving the tense figure. The other man dropped the knife in front of Lucas, who said something else and kicked the blade out into the street beyond. A moment later the thief had vanished into the maze of twisting alleys.

When he seemed convinced the would-be attacker had truly disappeared, Lucas turned back to face Jessica, who still stood, her arms piled high with packages, her eyes still wide from fright. He stared at her for a very long moment and she had the impression he was struggling for self-control.

"Are you all right?" he finally grated in a voice that was far too civil. Lowering his eyes, he knelt to slip the knife back into his low-cut boot.

"Yes. Yes, I'm fine. A little scared, but otherwise okay." What was he thinking? Why wasn't he yelling at her? He must be furious with her for disobeying his order and going off by herself to explore the far corners of the market. If the situation had been reversed, she would have been tearing a wide strip off the offender! Hadn't Lucas warned her that parts of town were very unsafe? Jessica lowered her lashes anxiously as he came toward her, preparing herself for the tirade to come. "Lucas, I'm sorry, I didn't..."

"Forget it," he got out very carefully, reaching to take some of the packages. "Are you hungry?"

"Hungry? Well, I was a few minutes ago," she acknowledged uneasily. Why didn't he get it over? Why wasn't he reading her the riot act? She could feel the palpable tension in him, could almost touch the anger that she knew simmered just under the surface. He must be absolutely enraged at her stupidity!

"Good. I know an excellent little restaurant not too far from here," he said tightly. "I think we both need a place to sit down and cool off, don't you?"

Unable to think of anything to say to that, Jessica closed her mouth and walked silently beside him as he led the way out of the alley and back toward the main thoroughfare. Desperately she tried to figure out what was happening between them. If she had done something this stupid back in the desert, Lucas would have flayed her alive; she was positive of it.

Warily she darted him a questioning sideways glance, taking in the harsh set of his face as he walked alongside her. She had the distinct impression he was practically gritting his teeth to keep from yelling at her!

And then the truth hit her with the force of a lightning bolt. Lucas Kincaid, who had just successfully faced down a thief in an alley, who had been responsible for seeing himself and seven others safely through the aftermath of a plane crash, and who had helped patrol the dangerous streets of Los Angeles for eight years, was afraid to give her the simple tongue-lashing she undoubtedly deserved!

It was ludicrous, Jessica decided dazedly. The man had nerves of iron to match his eyes, and yet he didn't quite dare to vent his wrath on her! Was he really so terrified of angering her? Had she intimidated him so completely?

The confusion that that thought created in her mind kept Jessica silent until they had been seated in a small café. She remained silent as Lucas gave their order in a tightly controlled tone of voice that totally subdued the otherwise garrulous waitress.

Finally Jessica could stand it no longer. Impulsively she reached across the table and touched his hand. He glanced down at her fingers lying over his whitened knuckles and then up at her repentant expression. "Lucas, you were right. I should never have ventured off on my own like that. My only excuse is that I never intended to wander so far. One thing led to another and I just…" She broke off, unable to think of any reasonable excuse under the circumstances. "Thank you," she concluded more firmly. "I was never so relieved to see anyone in my life as I was to see you standing at the entrance of that alley!"

He took a deep, steadying breath and she sensed some of the tension leave his hard frame. His eyes cleared a little and the large hand she had been touching curled around her fingers with just the smallest hint of violence.

"The important thing is that you're all right," he tried to say gallantly. Jessica knew he wanted to say a great deal more that was a great deal less than gallant, and she hid an inward smile when he so obviously bit it back. "Please, Jessie, don't ever do that to me again!"

"No, Lucas," she promised, meaning it.

He relaxed a little further as they ate spicy enchiladas and tacos and by the time they started back to the ship, Lucas was almost back to normal. Jessica kept a wary eye on him from time to time and it came to her that she probably would have felt better if he had given in to the flaring temper that had gripped

him. A streak of self-honesty forced her to admit she
certainly deserved a stern lecture at the least. He probably would have felt much better afterward, too.

But he was too nervous of alienating her to risk it.
Incredible. Jessica wondered at that knowledge again
and again during the course of the long, hot afternoon.
Lucas wanted her good will so badly he had clamped
down on his own perfectly natural reaction to her in-
excusable actions.

Another piece of surprising self-knowledge struck
Jessica later as he left her at her stateroom door to
dress for dinner. She glanced in the mirror as she an-
alyzed it critically.

It was difficult to define, but it had something to do
with her own emotions when Lucas had arrived to rescue her. She had experienced more than the natural
and overwhelming relief. It was something beyond
gratitude, too.

It had something to do with the fact that she had a
claim on his protection. When she had looked up to
find him standing in the alley, prepared to defend her,
Jessica had known a fierce feeling of rightness about
the situation. He would take care of her. Because she
belonged to him?

With a tight-lipped uneasiness, Jessica pushed that
thought out of her mind and reached for the dress she
intended to wear to dinner.

Seven

The message from Raul Estrada was waiting for Jessica at the purser's desk that evening. On the way into dinner with Lucas, she picked it up, slitting open the small white envelope curiously.

"From someone in Acapulco?" Lucas inquired, unabashedly trying to read over her shoulder, which was delightfully bared by the halter-necked, peacock-toned gown she wore.

"Raul Estrada. He's the manager of the Scanlon hotel here in Acapulco. He's apparently learned from someone at headquarters in L.A. that I'm on board this ship and is inviting me to spend tomorrow at the hotel." She lifted her eyes from the small note and smiled. "That will work out perfectly, won't it?" Lucas just looked at her, his gaze shuttered, and Jessica went on very brightly. "We don't sail until tomorrow evening and it would be interesting to see the local operation. I'll send word that we'll be happy to accept the invitation. Raul is an excellent host."

"He should be," Lucas observed sardonically as he took her arm and continued toward the dining room. "It's his profession, isn't it?"

"You've got a point," Jessica laughed. "You'd like to go, then?"

"I'll go. Have you met this Estrada character before?"

"Oh, yes. I've run into him occasionally at regional Scanlon meetings. He's very charming."

"A member of the family, in other words?" Lucas murmured dryly as they took their seats and greeted the Howards.

"Definitely." Jessica's smile was a little too brilliant, holding almost a hint of challenge. Lucas did not attempt to respond to it.

In fact, he remained unusually quiet throughout dinner, managing a minimum of polite conversation with Ann and Bill Howard, but little else. He eyed Jessica's order of *seviche* suspiciously, but refrained from commenting on the popular South American concoction, which consisted of raw scallops, onions, and peppers drenched in lime juice. Jessica found herself missing his teasing remarks about her choice of food. Was he still brooding about the scene in Acapulco that afternoon?

When he kissed her goodnight at her stateroom door later that evening and then turned to stride off down the carpeted corridor to his own deck, Jessica was thoroughly perplexed. She had spent most of the day in excited anticipation of how the night would end. It had never occurred to her that she wouldn't be waking in Lucas's arms the next morning.

Confused and unexpectedly annoyed by the turn of events, she shut the door behind him with undue force and locked it. If he wanted to sulk because he hadn't dared chew her out for her behavior earlier in the day, that was his problem!

Raul Estrada sent a car for them the next morning after breakfast. It was waiting on the dock when the ship's tender deposited its first load of passengers.

"I thought perhaps you might have changed your mind about coming with me this morning, Lucas," Jessica remarked a little coolly as she climbed into the back seat of the chauffeured black Mercedes with the Scanlon crest on the door.

"I wouldn't have missed this opportunity for the world," Lucas told her politely as the chauffeur shut the door crisply and slid into the driver's seat. "After all, it's a chance to get an inside look at your world. That's the Scanlon hotel at the far end of the beach, isn't it?"

From the pleasant coolness of the air-conditioned car, Jessica glanced out and saw, far in the distance, the familiar Scanlon symbol on top of a huge, white gleaming tower. "Yes, that's the slice of the Scanlon world here in Acapulco. I keep telling you, Lucas," she added, with a tiny smile, "it's a very enjoyable world. Careful you don't get seduced by it."

He turned his head to give her a sober, straight glance. "I can be seduced only by you, Jessie. Not a hotel."

She swallowed under the impact of his gaze. "Really?'' she managed very bravely, ''I didn't notice that you were, uh, overcome last night!'' Damn! What had made her say that?

But Lucas's hard mouth, which hadn't smiled much thus far that morning began to curve into a suddenly indulgent smile. ''Last night I had to work a few things out in my head. Miss me?''

Goaded, Jessica glared at him. ''I'm hardly likely to admit a thing like that, am I?'' Then, determined to produce an airy counterattack, she went on lightly. ''What were you working out in your head, Lucas? All the things you didn't quite dare to say after you rescued me in that alley?''

''Was it so obvious?'' he groaned wryly.

Impulsively Jessica patted his leg. ''Don't worry, Lucas. I called myself every name in the book. I was probably harder on me than you would have been! Consider the riot act as having been read. Let's just forget the whole thing, shall we?''

He slanted her an oblique glance, ignoring her touch. ''What would you have done if I'd lost my temper yesterday, Jessie?''

''Probably lost mine in turn! This way you managed to make me feel terribly guilty. Much more effective, I'm sure.'' She grinned.

''Does it strike you that you're becoming a little condescending?''

She heard the thin edge of sharpened steel under the words and withdrew her hand from his leg immediately. Then she went very still for a moment as her eyes locked with his. ''It strikes me,'' she stated very carefully, ''that I'm trying to make a joke out of the tension caused by yesterday's unfortunate occurrence. If you'd rather not take that approach then by all means start screaming abuse at me. I'm sure the chauffeur will be happy to turn around and take you back to the ship.''

The atmosphere inside the Mercedes was suddenly charged with the full force of their silent clash of wills. Jessica sat tensely, knowing she would win, because there was no option for Lucas other than to back down. She knew that, but even so she couldn't prevent an inward sigh of relief when he nodded his head.

''I agree. Let's forget it,'' he said quietly. ''Tell me about Raul Estrada.''

Jessica accepted the surrender graciously. What else could the man have done under the circumstances? She smiled with warmth and enthusiasm as the heavy car slowed in front of the ornate hotel entrance.

''You'll see for yourself in a minute. There he is now.''

Raul Estrada came down the tiled steps, skirted the huge fountain in the center of the drive, and strode toward the car with a gleaming smile of urbane welcome on his handsome face. He was nearly forty and there was the smallest hint of a paunch beneath the immaculately tailored white tropical jacket he wore, but the handsome, dark face bequeathed to him by his Spanish ancestors remained well molded and attractive. He greeted Jessica as she stepped out of the car with a kiss which, by a deft twist of her head, she managed to place on her cheek, and perfect, California-accented English. Raul was totally bilingual.

''Jessie, my dear! It's so good to see you again. You

certainly gave everyone a scare last week. We heard about the plane crash all the way down here! When I learned from Paul Tanner in L.A. that you were sailing down to Acapulco, I took a chance and called the ship in the harbor. Ah! And this is the gentleman you said would accompany you. A friend of Jessie's is always welcome, señor!''

"I'm close to Jessie, but I'm not sure you could really call me a friend of the family," Lucas murmured, obligingly taking the proffered palm and shaking it firmly as he eyed the other man.

Raul blinked uncertainly. "I beg your pardon?"

"A little joke, Raul," Jessica put in quickly as she made introductions. "Nothing important. What a lovely facility," she added gaily, surveying the beautiful building. "Scanlon certainly did itself proud here in Acapulco. I so wanted to come down for the opening ceremonies a year ago, but I couldn't get away at the time."

Raul beamed proudly as all Scanlon managers tended to do when someone complimented the hotels they managed. "Come inside, both of you. I have arranged for lunch later. I thought perhaps you might enjoy seeing the hotel first, though, eh, Jessie?" He smiled at her expectantly.

"Naturally. I'm sure Lucas will enjoy a backstage tour, too."

"'Know the enemy,' that's my motto," Lucas murmured just loud enough for Jessica to hear. "Yes, I would appreciate a tour of the facilities."

"Good, good, right this way, then," Raul commanded cheerfully. "We'll start with the grounds."

He led the way through the circular, open-air lobby with its gleaming brass and tile toward the inviting gardens, which faced the beach.

In spite of his rather sarcastic comment, Lucas did, indeed, appear fascinated with the detailed tour they received. "You have your own water purification plant?" he asked at one point as they walked through the kitchens.

"We want the tourists to feel perfectly comfortable about any water used within the hotel, whether it be in the restaurant or the bar or the shower. It is simpler and more reliable to process all the water in the building to ensure that it is clean than to rely on the city facilities. In some of the smaller hotels, bottled water must be provided in every room. American tourists don't care for that! They keep forgetting and turning on the tap."

"Nothing but the best from Scanlon," Jessica chuckled.

"So I'm continually reminded," Lucas growled.

They followed Raul through the tropical grounds to view the two swimming pools, one of which had a built-in bar at one end where guests sat on stools in the water and sipped fruit-based drinks served by bartenders on the other side of a barrier. The other pool had been designed to closely resemble a jungle pool, complete with artificial waterfall. Tourists luxuriated in the elegant environs, soaking up the sun and spending a great deal of money on cooling drinks.

"We try to ensure that everything a visitor could wish is housed under the Scanlon roof. Shops, sports, the beach, nightclubs, and three restaurants—all are provided," Raul explained to Lucas as they concluded the tour and walked toward a private garden terrace which overlooked the sea.

"'Scanlon is a world apart,'" Jessica quoted from a company brochure.

"A fantasy world," Lucas put in meaningfully. "Nice for a vacation, but surely a little cloying to live in all the time? It's like the ship we're on."

It was Raul who responded with a laugh and a conspiratorial wink at Jessica as he seated them in his private garden and signaled a nearby white-coated waiter who stood in readiness. "Scanlon makes it well worth our while to live in a gilded cage, doesn't it, Jessie?"

"Very much so," she responded, meeting Lucas's narrowed eyes.

It was Lucas who looked away. "Are you married, Raul? Does your wife share this, uh, cage with you?"

There was a short pause and then Raul said quietly, his dark eyes on Jessica, "My wife died some years ago, Lucas. I have not, as yet, remarried."

Lucas glanced from Raul's face to Jessica's cool features. "But when you do it will be within the family?" he suggested deliberately.

"I'm afraid I don't understand." Raul finally glanced back at his guest as the waiter brought in a fresh-fruit salad sprinkled with coconut.

"I meant you would prefer to marry a Scanlon employee if you were to remarry?" Lucas persisted even though Jessica had begun to frown at him from the other side of the table.

Raul smiled at once and nodded. "The idea has its

merits, hasn't it, Jessie? Just imagine how happy Scanlon would be to have someone like you marry someone like me, hmmm? In one fell swoop they would have all the basic management needs of the hotel covered by a husband-and-wife team!''

Jessica forced a light laugh, her feminine intuition warning her that this was more than a casual conversation, at least on Lucas's part. With a firm hand she turned the discussion in another direction, inquiring about Raul's current staffing needs and problems.

For the remainder of lunch the tactic seemed to work. Lucas participated occasionally in the conversation, but for the most part he seemed to watch Raul's face as if he were studying the man. It made Jessica increasingly uneasy. It was as if she'd brought a wild animal to the table and now had to live with the knowledge that it might choose to dine off one of the guests instead of what was placed before it on a plate.

Over and over again she told herself that that was ridiculous. Lucas wouldn't, he *couldn't* do anything too awful. Could he? But she didn't care for the way he patiently watched the older man. After lunch, when Raul temporarily excused himself on a matter that had arisen at the front desk, she told Lucas as much.

''You keep staring at him!'' she hissed as they strolled through one of the lush gardens. ''It's embarrassing.''

''Sorry.''

''You're not sorry! What's the matter with you, anyway? He's our host!''

''He's thinking what an asset you'd be to his career," Lucas countered easily, pausing beside a huge bloom to inhale the scent.

"What?" she squeaked. "That's ridiculous!" But she glanced away quickly as he turned to stare at her.

"No, it's not. And what's more you knew it before we even accepted the invitation, didn't you? How well do you know Raul Estrada, Jessie?" Lucas asked in a cool voice.

"I told you, we've met on a few occasions over the years..."

"Tell me something," Lucas interrupted interestedly, "does the idea of being married for business reasons appeal to you?"

"That doesn't deserve an answer!"

"Does he know exactly how good a deal he'd be getting? That you're not only good in business but that you're also good in..."

"Don't say it, Lucas, I'm warning you!" she snapped before he could finish the sentence.

He held her cold eyes for a second longer and then sighed. "I'm sorry, Jessie. I'm jealous as hell."

Instantly she was contrite. How could this man manage to infuriate her one moment and then make her anxious to forgive him the next? "Lucas, there's nothing to be concerned about. If you want the truth, I know that Raul would not be adverse to marrying me. It's been hinted at before. But he'd never push it unless I encouraged him." She hastened on quickly, seeing Lucas's gaze darken. "He's very much the gentleman!"

"Unlike me?" Lucas growled sardonically.

A slow smile crept across her face. "Oh, I don't

know. You've been behaving yourself fairly decently lately. Come on, let's go back to the main lobby. Raul should be finished with his business soon.''

She turned to start back along the path, but came to an abrupt halt as Lucas stretched out a hand and snagged her by the wrist. "Jessie," he said very seriously as she looked back at him with an inquiringly lifted eyebrow, "I'm going to take you away from all this."

"Back to the ship, you mean?" she taunted lightly, alarmed by the sudden rush of excitement in her veins and by the degree of certainty in his set face.

"No, that's just more of the same," he said impatiently. "We'll finish the cruise, all right, but when we get back I'm going to give you a place where you can be a woman as well as a prized hotel executive. A place where you'll know beyond any doubt that you're wanted for yourself, not just because you'll advance a man's career. We'll make our own reality, you and I, Jessie Travers. You're going to come and live with me."

Aquamarine eyes wide and startled, her heart pounding the way it had the day before when she'd been trapped in the alley, Jessie stared at him, speechless. This wasn't the way she had planned it. Lucas held an attraction for her, she could not deny it, but she certainly had no intention of giving in to it so completely. She had only wanted to prove that she could conduct the relationship on her own terms. Hadn't she?

Scrambling for a response to the unexpected move he had just made, Jessica smiled with belated perception. "It's not really Raul you're jealous of, is it? It's Scanlon."

"Do you blame me? You've made that company your life, your family and your world!"

And he saw no lasting place for himself in that world, Jessica realized. Well, what had he expected? "So I'm absorbed in my job. Is that so bad? Weren't you wrapped up in your work with the police department? I've always heard that that particular profession demands everything from an individual. The department becomes the most important thing in life."

"It was a prison of a job, all right, but at least it was an honest prison," he gritted. "One can see the bars for what they are and for some people, like me, it becomes obvious that escape is the only answer. But you don't even want to acknowledge your own pretty cage. Scanlon has brainwashed you!"

"That's not true!"

"It's given you a perfect outlet for the naturally aggressive, dynamic side of your nature and you've rushed to grab it. If you had another side to your life, that wouldn't be so bad. But somehow you've lost your options or cut them off. Have you ever been in love, Jessie?" he concluded harshly. "Have you ever really come alive in a man's arms the way you do in mine? Is that why you're so afraid of me? Because I'm opening doors that you're afraid to walk through?"

"Stop it, Lucas!" she blazed.

"Are you afraid of me?" he persisted, surveying her critically, as if he would find the answer in her cold, angry, yet composed face.

"Should I be?" she bit out scathingly.

"Perhaps," he said. "I'm a threat to your neat, charming little world, aren't I? But maybe you haven't fully realized that yet."

"You have no business threatening me! If you don't stop it this minute, I swear, I'll..."

"Jessie," he whispered, tugging her rigid figure into his arms. "I'm sorry. I didn't mean to frighten you."

"I'm not frightened, damn it!" she muttered fiercely into his shirt.

But he held her there in the garden for a few minutes as if she had been very frightened, indeed, and Jessica's tense body slowly began to relax. His hands gentled her and Jessica told herself the only emotion he was successfully soothing away was her extreme sense of irritation. Certainly not fear. She did not fear Lucas Kincaid. Not here in her world.

"Is this a form of apology?" she finally got out dryly.

"Something like that, I suppose. I didn't meant to upset you, honey. You know that, don't you?" He pulled away to search her eyes. "I'm trying so damn hard to be on my best behavior!"

The earnest entreaty in his face brought Jessica's sense of humor back to life. Poor Lucas. How much more of this frustration with her would he take before he realized he wasn't ever again going to find the woman he'd found so briefly out there in the desert?

"I know, Lucas, I know." Then she summoned up a small grin. "But don't you realize it's not terribly modern to be jealous of a woman's job?"

"I won't be after I know for certain you'll be coming home to me at night and not to a hotel room!'' he told her confidently, his large hands moving with unconscious sensuality on her shoulders.

"Lucas,'' she protested, realizing he was deadly serious, ''please don't push me like this. We have no commitment to each other and you have no right to talk as if we do!''

"Okay, honey, calm down. I know you aren't ready for a commitment yet.''

"Most definitely not! I'm on vacation, remember?'' she parried, using her brightest, most dazzling smile to hide her inner uncertainty. ''I'm recuperating from five miserable days spent in a desert!''

"Were they really so miserable?'' he questioned gently.

"From my point of view, yes! Or did you somehow gain the impression I actually enjoyed washing clothes by hand in a stream and eating bunnies four nights in a row?'' she demanded flippantly.

"Jessie, this isn't the first time you've made a joke about the experience. Don't you see that it can't have been that devastating for you if you can laugh about it now?''

Jessica considered that briefly. ''As I said before, time and distance always add perspective. Now that I'm back in the real world I am able to see the more amusing side of things. I've regained my equilibrium, I suppose. Shows what a few good meals and a dose of Scanlon-oriented reality can do for a person!'' Her eyes lit with mischief. ''But, Lucas, you must understand that the reason I can laugh about washing your clothes in a desert stream is that I know the odds are vastly in favor of my never having to do it again, not because it was intrinsically enjoyable or amusing!''

"Jessie, what you and I had together in that desert *was* real.''

"No," she denied, turning her face toward the ocean. "It had nothing to do with reality. Come on, Lucas, Raul will be waiting.''

As the time for their departure drew near, Raul seemed to create an increasingly intimate air between himself and Jessica. He did nothing overt, merely assumed a sense of familiarity, which somehow managed to continually exclude Lucas.

Aware of Lucas's growing tension, Jessica tried resolutely to lighten the situation. She knew she could handle Raul Estrada, but Lucas didn't seem to know it. As the afternoon progressed, she found herself trying to pacify him in subtle ways.

"I'll be in L.A. next month, Jessie," Raul announced calmly as they sat chatting on the scented terrace outside his luxuriously furnished apartment. "You will be in town, won't you?" he asked suavely.

"As far as I know," Jessica responded, conscious of Lucas's hardening glance as he toyed with his glass of iced coffee. "I'll be back at work in another week and there will undoubtedly be a lot of catching up to do."

"Excellent! We'll make it a point to get together for dinner then, hmmm?"

"Uh, perhaps." Belatedly Jessica saw the cold iron in Lucas's gaze. "I'm going to be rather busy for most of the summer, though," she heard herself add quickly. "Several major conventions, including a political affair, are booked. You know what those are like!''

''Ah, yes. But I'm sure there will be time for us,'' Raul noted gently. ''How is Sam, by the way? Is he still in charge of L.A. food and beverage?''

''Yes and as far as I know he's fine.'' Warily Jessica eyed Lucas; he hadn't said a word for the past twenty minutes. It was like waiting for a volcano to blow, she thought disgustedly. Perhaps she'd better see about getting him out of there before the sky fell. The last thing she wanted was to have him embarrass her in front of another Scanlon employee!

''Raul, it's been great seeing you again,'' she began firmly, setting down her glass of coffee, ''but I think it's time Lucas and I got back to the ship. I seem to recall the captain saying over the loudspeaker this morning that his ship would wait for no one when sailing time arrived!''

''Not even a Scanlon employee,'' Lucas drawled, restlessly getting to his feet.

Whatever Raul Estrada might have said in response was lost as the peaceful quiet was suddenly interrupted by a short, sharp yip from an excited dog. Automatically all three people glanced toward a nearby hedge just as a scrawny, tan mutt came flying through. It paused a moment to examine the three humans and then bounded happily toward Jessica, floppy ears bouncing.

''Where the devil did that creature come from?'' Raul muttered in annoyance. ''I'll have Fernando get rid of him. There are so many strays here in Acapulco! All my employees have instructions to keep them off the grounds, but occasionally one slips through. Be careful, Jessie, he'll get your white slacks filthy.''

Amused at the dog's unabashed enthusiasm, Jessica leaned down to pat him carefully on the head. It was the wrong thing to do. The cheerful animal chose to interpret the sign as one of welcome and, with a joyous bark, reared up to plant muddy paws squarely on the front of the pristine white slacks.

''Oh, no!'' Jessica laughed ruefully, going ahead and petting the dog, anyway.

Instantly Raul was at her side, aiming a well-shod foot at the offending animal.

''Hey!'' Lucas objected harshly, starting forward with a frown. He needn't have worried. The tan dog had survived long enough on the handouts of Acapulco tourists to have learned something about human nature. He had encountered Raul's approach often enough. With a quick twist of his thin body, the animal avoided the kick, dodging around behind Jessica. An instant later, Lucas reached him and swept him safely up under one arm.

Knowing a sucker when he saw one, the dog enthusiastically began to lick Lucas's face. ''Jessie and I are on our way out. We'll see that the dog is removed from your fantasy world, Estrada!''

''As you wish,'' Raul replied, losing interest as he turned back to Jessica. ''I am sorry about the damage done to your clothing, my dear.''

Jessica shook her head in easy dismissal. ''Forget it. I've endured worse. Remember the time the assistant chef dumped an entire kettle of hollandaise down the front of my gown just before that important dinner in San Francisco last year? I assure you I'll survive a couple of paw prints." She glanced over at Lucas. He still held the wriggling dog, which was still madly attempting to lick its benefactor's face.

All might have gone well at that point if Raul hadn't presumed a little too far. "Goodbye, Jessie," he murmured, ignoring Lucas to bend forward and kiss Jessica full on her surprised mouth. "I will definitely see you next month. Be sure to hold several evenings free for me, my dear."

Startled by the unexpected degree of affection from a man she'd always thought of as a business friend, Jessica stepped back and opened her lips to say something very noncommittal.

She never got the chance. Lucas was moving toward her, the dog tucked under one arm, his free hand extended to grasp Jessica's wrist. Roughly he spoke to Raul. The harsh, uncompromising stream of Spanish which flowed from his lips was cold and lethal, even to Jessica's ears, and she didn't have the faintest idea of what was being said. The impact on Raul, however, was immediate and obvious.

The older man fell back a pace, astonished, as Lucas finished speaking and yanked abruptly on his captive's hand. Dog and woman safely chained to him, he started toward the exit.

"Jessie!" Raul called after her retreating figure. "What's going on? Is what he just said true?"

"Is what true?" Unable to free herself, Jessica stumbled a little as she tried to glance back at her friend. Lucas never looked back and never slackened his forward momentum.

"Do you belong to him?" Raul called anxiously. "He says you are his woman!"

Shocked, Jessica tried to summon a hasty protest, but it was too late. Lucas hauled them around the corner and then they were hurrying through the elegant, airy lobby, causing amused and curious expressions to appear on the faces of clerks and guests alike.

Outside Lucas tossed his companions into the back seat of a waiting cab and climbed in beside them, shutting the door with a vicious slam and issuing quick instructions in Spanish to the obliging driver.

Then he leaned back in the seat and turned to meet Jessica's accusing gaze. The dog was happily ensconced on her lap, completing the ruination of the white slacks, and she unthinkingly lifted a hand to pat its dirty, tan fur.

"How dare you?" she hissed at Lucas. "If you were an employee of mine I'd have you fired for embarrassing me like that! How dare you make such an unforgivable scene! Raul Estrada is a friend of mine; nothing more—and even if he were something more, that still wouldn't give you the right to behave so outrageously!"

"He shouldn't have tried to kick the dog and kiss you." Lucas sank more deeply into the battered seat as the cab rocketed toward the docks. "I was doing okay up to that point. God knows I wanted to tell him to keep his hands off you often enough during the day, but I knew you'd be furious."

"I am furious! You had absolutely no right to tell him such things!"

"That you're my woman?" Lucas slanted her an

iron glance and then refocused his attention on the colorful street scene outside the car's window. "It's the truth, Jessie. You only seem willing to admit it when you're in my arms, but it's the truth and you know it."

"It is not the truth! Damn it, Lucas, if the whole thing weren't so ludicrous, I'd hire someone to skin you alive! I have never been so furious in my life!"

"Jessie," he said placatingly, "I'm sorry about what happened. If you'd just gotten us out of there a little earlier…"

"So it's my fault, is it?"

"Well, yes, in a way. I know you think you can handle Estrada, but you weren't doing a very good job there toward the end. You were practically promising to meet him next month in Los Angeles!"

"I fully intend to meet him. I shall be looking forward to it, in fact! It will be a pleasure to go out with a gentleman!"

"Honey, don't say things like that. You're just upset," he soothed.

"You're impossible," she groaned, some of her anger seeping out of her as the dog on her lap swiped her cheek with his tongue and looked at her with such hope in his eyes she couldn't resist him. "Your dog is hungry. What are you going to do about him? We can't take him on board ship!"

"I know. We'll stop and buy him some tacos before we turn him loose. He'll survive, as long as he steers clear of Estrada's perfect garden!" There was a significant pause. "Jessie, I'm sorry I embarrassed you."

"Are you, Lucas?" she asked tightly.

"Sweetheart, we were making so much progress," he murmured pleadingly. "Please don't ruin it all now because of what just happened back there at the hotel!"

"Progress!" she exploded, turning the full force of her glowering gaze on him. "*Progress!* Is that what you thought was happening?"

"You know it was," he said levelly. "You were beginning to see the other side of me. You were getting over some of your anger and you were even starting to laugh at some of the things that happened back there in the desert!" He broke off to narrow his eyes at her as she began to chuckle softly. "What's so amusing?" he demanded stiffly.

"You are, Lucas," she managed wickedly. "For thinking you were making progress with me."

"Jessie," he began on a sudden note of warning.

"Lucas, I'm the one who was making progress with you. Or thought I was. It's obvious there are still some rough spots." She grinned.

He didn't move, but his eyes were suddenly watchful and the grooves at the edge of his mouth tightened. "What are you trying to say, Jessie?" he asked very softly.

"Isn't it obvious? I'm conducting an affair with you, Lucas Kincaid," she murmured with saccharine sweetness. "On my terms, not yours. And for future reference, please take note of the fact that I do not want you flying off the handle and making wild claims every time another man sees fit to be nice to me. Is that understood?"

But even as she spoke the haughty, arrogant words, Jessica was regretting them.

Eight

Unfortunately, the feeling of regret didn't disappear. Why had she let her temper get the better of her? Jessica asked herself that question for the rest of the afternoon and was still asking it as she dressed for dinner.

Surely she had only told him the truth, she argued with herself. Hadn't she already proven whatever it was she had set out to prove? A long-term affair had never been a goal of hers, anyway, so what did it matter if her precipitous words had ended the situation sooner than she had expected? She ought to be content with having made her point in no uncertain terms and then letting Lucas off her hook. He hadn't really deserved to be misled for very long.

When all was said and done, Lucas Kincaid was an honest, straightforward man. Jessica knew first-hand that she could trust him with her life. Still, he'd pushed her into her defensive posture. He was the one who'd followed her on board the ship and set out to ruin her vacation!

But she hadn't meant to hurt him. She'd only wanted to put him in his place. Well, she had done that this afternoon in the taxi and she was still feeling an emotion suspiciously like guilt. Jessica chewed her lip in an agony of frustration as she pulled the little black dress from the small stateroom closet. The frustration and the guilt had been building steadily ever since that scene in the taxi, and they weren't pleasant sensations. She should have been feeling satisfaction, not remorse!

Perhaps if he'd lost his own temper and raged at her in turn she might have felt better about her own taunting words; more justified, at least. As it was, Lucas had merely stared at her for a long moment, his expression totally unreadable, and then he'd asked the driver to find a place where they could buy food for the dog.

The creature had last been seen happily wolfing down several spicy tamales on a sidewalk as the taxi driver, shaking his head over the actions of the crazy gringos, drove Jessica and Lucas on to the docks.

Jessica hadn't seen Lucas for the rest of the afternoon and had told herself several times that it didn't matter. Now, as she slipped into the dashing little dress, she acknowledged that it did matter. "You're not supposed to be cruel to people who rescue little dogs," she announced to her image in the mirror. Tonight she would face him and explain what she had been doing and why. Then she would apologize and that would be the end of the matter. She really didn't *owe* him an apology, but maybe it would relieve her own gnawing sense of guilt if she gave him one. After all, whatever she'd had to prove to herself had been proven. Surely Lucas would no longer be interested in pursuing a relationship when he understood what she had been doing. She could end the whole thing tonight. It was messy, but at least this time they would be parting as equals.

How would Lucas react to her explanation? she wondered as she brushed her hair into a gleaming coil at the nape of her neck. Would he understand why she had acted as she did? That he had more or less pushed her into it by following her on board? Damn it! She was beginning to feel toward him the way he'd felt toward that small dog when Raul had attempted to kick the creature: protective.

Her emotions were in an incredibly complex tangle, she realized. There was a simple explanation, of course: Out in the desert she had been playing out of her league; here in her civilized, safe world, Lucas had been playing out of his. Neither one of them had wanted to hurt the other. Jessica straightened her shoulders determinedly as she left the stateroom. Tonight she would explain everything and put an end to the matter. That was assuming she could find him, she added wryly. Where had Lucas been keeping himself since they had returned from the Scanlon hotel?

He wandered into the dining room right on time, however, dark hair still damp from a shower, eyes cool and remote as they had been in the taxi. The Howards appeared to notice nothing particularly out of the ordinary. Perhaps they were growing accustomed to the unpredictable tension that flowed between their two tablemates.

In any event, they made the necessary dinner conversation, telling tales of what they had seen and done and bought in Acapulco.

"And how about you two?" Bill wound up jovially, as dessert was served.

Jessica nibbled her Brie as the others dug into apple pie, and attempted a small smile. "We saved a small dog from a terrible fate." Her eyes caught Lucas's cool gaze, inviting him to join in that humor. "Or rather Lucas did."

The Howards laughed good-naturedly as she gave a highly expurgated version of the story. Lucas listened to the light tale without comment, concentrating on his apple pie. Jessica couldn't tell if he was angry or simply bored. What in the world was he thinking? Was he sulking again?

That last notion pushed her into trying to goad him out of his self-imposed silence. "I suppose the urge to rescue little dogs in distress is an occupational hazard which comes with being a pet shop owner?"

He looked up and she had the feeling his thoughts had been on something else entirely. "It was also an occupational hazard while I was a cop," he remarked and went back to his pie.

Jessica's eyes narrowed in astonishment as she realized he had just given her a major clue to what had led him to quit the LAPD. He had said he was a victim of job burnout, but she hadn't prodded any more deeply at the time. Now she knew what had led to that burnout. Lucas Kincaid, she was willing to bet, had grown frustrated and angry at being unable to save all the small, helpless people he was supposed to protect.

The flash of insight unnerved her, making it impossible to pick up the thread of the conversation and take it firmly in another direction. Fortunately, Ann Howard plunged to the rescue with a frivolous remark about the silver she had managed to find in what she hoped was a reliable shop in Acapulco. Jessica finished the excellent, perfectly ripened Brie without tasting the expensive cheese at all.

Lucas remained quiet for the rest of the meal, finishing his coffee in silence. But the inevitable could not be put off indefinitely. If he wasn't going to give her an opening, Jessica decided gamely, she would have to take the initiative. As he rose to leave the dining room, she did the same and placed her fingertips lightly but firmly on the sleeve of his corduroy jacket.

"I'd like to talk to you," Jessica murmured.

He glanced down at her hand and then nodded once. "Yes."

Without a word he led her out onto the upper deck, just as the ship's engines thrummed to life. They were under way again. The next port on the way back to Los Angeles would be Mazatlán. Jessica stood beside Lucas at the rail, watching the lights of Acapulco slowly recede. She took the moment to gather herself for what she had to say.

"I'm sorry, Lucas."

He didn't move. With one foot hooked on the bottom rail, he leaned forward, resting on his elbows, and watched the shoreline. The balmy breeze ruffled his hair and the faint light from the ship cast his face into a hard, unreadable profile. Determined to get the scene over and done with as efficiently as possible, Jessica took another breath.

"When I saw you again after the accident all I could think about was how I didn't want to be reminded of what had happened out there in the desert. When you insisted on trying to reestablish a relationship, I decided I would use the opportunity to prove to myself that here in the real world I wouldn't react to you the way I had after the crash. Here you wouldn't be able to dominate me and if we went to bed together it would be as equals."

"With you being a little more equal than me?" he interposed softly.

Jessica slid a sideways glance at his face as she stood stiffly beside him. What was he thinking? Damn it! She couldn't tell if he was depressed, furious, or totally uncaring about the whole situation!

"Perhaps," she admitted in a voice that was every bit as cool as the one he had used.

"Revenge?" he suggested mildly, apparently undisturbed by the notion.

Jessica's mouth firmed as he asked her the question she had asked herself earlier. "No, it was far more complicated than that, I think. But that may have been a part of it. I was more interested in trying to prove something to myself than in trying to punish you, though. Do you see the difference?"

"And now?" he prompted.

He hadn't answered her question, she realized

wryly. Here she was attempting to explain, even apologize, and he was already beginning to arouse her irritation again. Deliberately?

"I knew this afternoon that what I wanted to prove had already been established. In my world I can handle you, Lucas. I'm not boasting. It's the simple truth. I think you've known that all along, haven't you? You can't treat me the way you did out on the desert. Back here in civilization there are rules which neither of us can ignore. The point has been made. There's no reason to drag it out any further."

"You've had enough revenge?" he queried blandly.

"It wasn't revenge! At least, not all of it. That's what I'm trying to explain," she snapped. "Damn it, Lucas, don't be deliberately obtuse!"

"To explain something, you first have to understand it completely yourself," he noted idly.

"I do understand it! I'm saying I've satisfied myself and now I want to call the whole thing off. I don't want to punish you, Lucas!"

"Why not?"

Jessica sighed. "Because you're basically a sincere, honest man. Even a compassionate one. You've never attempted to deceive me. You're not really guilty of anything criminal or vicious. We were both caught in a unique situation and it affected us in a way that we couldn't control. The situation, thank heaven, is highly unlikely to ever arise again. It left me feeling disgusted with myself, though, and when you showed up on this ship I felt very uncomfortable."

"So you decided to prove to yourself that here in

your fantasy world you aren't trapped the way you were out in the desert. Here you're safe.''

"Something like that. I'm glad you're beginning to understand, Lucas,'' she told him earnestly. "We both know that everything is different here in real life.''

"Do we?" His eyes were still on the receding shoreline, but Jessica's nerves suddenly tingled with unexpected warning.

"Of course,'' she affirmed as much to herself as to him. "Just look at the kid-glove treatment you've given me lately. A week ago if I'd disobeyed orders the way I did yesterday afternoon you would have done something very emphatic about it. Probably in front of all the others, too, as an example!'' She tried to inject just the proper amount of rueful humor into the words. "I knew the other night when we..." The next sentence trailed off weakly as a rush of warmth assailed her.

"When we made love?" he finished helpfully.

"Yes,'' she managed to get out, staring at the lights in the distance. "I knew then that everything was certainly normal again. I didn't feel as though I'd been... Oh, never mind, you know what I'm trying to say.'' She was glad the shadows hid the flush which was undoubtedly painting her throat and cheeks.

"You didn't feel as though you'd surrendered to the dominant male in the herd,'' he concluded dryly. "I believe that was how you described our first night together.''

"Lucas, do you understand what I'm trying to say?" she demanded with a hint of asperity. This had gone far enough. She'd apologized, even though there had been no real need, and she'd explained the motives behind her actions. She didn't owe him anything else. Lucas Kincaid might be a sincere and basically honest man, but he was also a thoroughly exasperating one!

He turned slowly at last to face her, continuing to lean negligently against the rail as he did so. For the first time that evening the shutters were opened and Jessica had a good look at the emotions he had been hiding for the past several hours.

The sight was enough to make her shiver in uneasy surprise. Good God! She had wondered what he was thinking all evening, but she hadn't expected this!

There was no sign that he had been sulking. There was also no indication that he had been hurt by her words. Nor was there anger in that abruptly clear gaze. Having expected some variation on those emotions, Jessica was totally unprepared for the piercing certainty with which he pinned her.

"I understand what you're trying to say, Jessie. But you haven't got the vaguest idea of what you're talking about." His mouth was edged with a faint, masculine humor which disturbed her as nothing else could have done. It said as clearly as his words that she had just made a fool out of herself.

"Lucas, I don't know what game you're playing, but I..."

"I'm not playing any games. You're the one who's been doing that, honey, and I think it's time we put a stop to them. You've been operating under a slight misconception, Jessie."

"What misconception?" she flared, the wariness

she thought long banished springing to life within her as if it had never been far below the surface. The knowledge angered her.

"The notion that everything's different between us just because you're back in your gilded cage. The reality of what happened between you and me, sweetheart, is independent of our environment. I was hoping that you'd come to that conclusion on your own, but it looks as if you've been using the time I gave you to 'prove' something to yourself. Apparently you've been so busy drawing stupid conclusions from my actions that you've overlooked one important fact."

"Which is?"

"Which is that you're no safer from me here in what you choose to call civilization than you were out in the desert." He made no move to touch her, but Jessica flinched and retreated a step as if he had. Her eyes widened and her lips parted in shock.

"No!" she whispered.

Lucas watched her with detached curiosity.

"You couldn't run fast enough to get back to the security of Scanlon, could you, Jessie? I'll bet you've never run from a man in your life the way you ran from me."

"I did not run!"

"You couldn't wait to get back inside your cage," he went on calmly, as if he were analyzing an interesting phenomenon. "Couldn't wait to slam the door in my face. I've been trying to coax you back outside, Jessie. Didn't you realize that? I know I've been treating you with kid gloves. I was hoping you'd relax and begin to feel more secure in my presence if I didn't push you too hard, too fast. I knew that what happened after the crash was something you weren't quite ready to accept. But I thought that, given a little time and not too much pressure, you'd see that what took place between us was real, not some form of strange, animalistic behavior for which you don't have to accept responsibility. I wanted you to open the cage door yourself, Jessie, but you're not going to do that, are you? You're going to hide inside and play sophisticated little games designed to make yourself feel secure and in control.''

''I'm not in a cage, Lucas, I'm in my own world, the *real* world, and there's nothing you can do to get me back out of it!'' she exclaimed, her fingers digging into the rail at her side as she faced him proudly.

''Well, it's obvious I'm not going to coax you out of it, I'll grant that,'' he admitted with surprising ease. ''But I've been giving it some serious thought since you made your position clear in the taxi this afternoon.''

Was that what he'd been dwelling on? she wondered frantically.

''Lucas, I don't know what momentous conclusion you've reached, but I do know this discussion has gone far enough. I've apologized for something which probably didn't merit an apology in the first place and I've...''

''It didn't. But you had to do it, didn't you? That's what comes of being soft under the surface, honey. You thought you'd made me suffer and you felt guilty. Poor Jessie. You thought you might have hurt me with your clever little plans, didn't you? Honey, you didn't crush me, you just made me realize I'm wasting my time with the walking-on-eggs approach. It might work eventually, but I'm not sure I'll last out the process now. When I found you in that alley yesterday it was all I could do not to turn you over my knee for having gotten yourself into such a stupid scrape. And this afternoon I thought I'd really lose control watching that slick Estrada oozing charm all over you. The dog saved both your necks, by the way, did you know that? It provided a reason to get you out of his garden before I lost my temper completely.''

"You said enough, as I recall!" she charged bitterly.

"You'll remember I did restrain myself to simply talking?" he murmured. "Still, it was an educational experience. If Estrada is the kind of man with whom you normally associate, I can see why falling for me must have been somewhat of a shock. After all, a man who has seen both sides of you, a man who knows who you really are is a threat, isn't he?"

"Damn you, Lucas, I'm not afraid of you!"

"Yes you are, and you're going to be even more afraid of me before you learn to accept the reality of our relationship. But there's no other way that I can see to manage things. I tried the gentling approach and you abused it.''

Jessica gasped in outrage at his interpretation of events. "Gentling! Lucas, I don't know where this is leading, but I swear, if you don't stop threatening me, I'll call a ship's officer!"

"I'm not threatening you, sweetheart," he soothed as if she were a fractious puppy. "And I'll be more than happy to enlighten you about where the conversation is leading. It's simple. I'm putting you on notice, Jessie. I'm through trying to persuade you to come back out of your gilded cage by yourself. I'm going to show you that the bars you think are protecting you are useless between us. You're not safe now that you're back in the Scanlon world. You're still as vulnerable to me as you ever were out in that desert because I'm still the man I was out there and you, thank God, are still the same woman. What happened between us is independent of time and circumstance. I'm going to reach into your safe little cage, honey, and pull you out into my arms.''

"Don't you dare touch me!" She stepped back another pace, thoroughly alarmed now.

"I won't. Not tonight," he drawled, straightening away from the rail. "Tonight I'm going to let you worry about the whole thing. You're an intelligent woman and with intelligence comes imagination. Use it, Jessie, to think about how far you can run on a ship this size.'' Strong, white teeth gleamed in a smile of savage amusement and then Lucas swung around on one heel and walked toward the entrance to the interior of the ship.

"I will never run from you or any other man," she couldn't resist calling after him.

"If you don't, things will end even sooner than I'd planned," he retorted mockingly, his hand on the door he was about to enter. "No, you'll run for a while. But eventually it's going to dawn on you that you're feeling the same things here in the middle of your so-called *real* world that you felt out in the desert. And when you make that connection, everything will be all right.''

Before she could catch her breath for a scathing response, Lucas was gone. Jessica stood staring after him, trying to assess what had happened to her. One thing was for certain, she decided irately, she no longer had to suffer any guilt over using him! Lucas had just threatened her, hadn't he? That made her the injured party! Or should that read *hunted* party?

That last thought sent another shiver through her. Hunted? Again? No, not here on this ship. He couldn't do such a thing to her!

Slowly Jessica left the rail, brows drawn together in a frown of intense concentration. The expression gave the strong, firm lines of her profile a look of cold severity in the moonlight. Unaware of where she was headed, Jessica walked slowly toward the bow of the ship. She was angry, restless, and confused, a combination potent enough to make a woman a little reckless. Deliberately she avoided the few other passengers who were out walking on deck.

There was a warmth and a freshness about the night air which put her too forcibly in mind of the clear desert nights she had known several days ago. It brought with it too many other associated memories. Dangerous memories.

He couldn't do this to her, Jessica told herself again and again as she stopped once more at the rail and stared down at the softly foaming water below. His latest campaign would only work if she were silly enough to let it work!

She was not the same unprotected female she had

been the last time. Surrounding her now were all the accoutrements of civilized society. She would be safe and she had already proven as much, hadn't she?

Spinning angrily around, Jessica fled the shadows of the quiet deck and went in search of laughter and company. She didn't want to ask herself why she needed the security of a crowd just then. The answer might have been too unnerving.

It wasn't hard to find what she sought. It all awaited her on the next deck down, where the lively dance band was entertaining in the largest of the three night-clubs. The defiant recklessness that had begun out on deck drove her to take a red leather stool at the bar, instead of a small table. It seemed important to find an escort for the evening and the direct approach was the quickest. Was she somehow looking for protection?

No! She merely wanted to enjoy the cruise. Coolly she ordered an after-dinner liqueur and swiveled halfway around on the stool to eye the crowded dance floor. One well-arched foot in a high-heeled black sandal swung in the manner of a prowling cat's tail.

Jessica didn't even see Lucas as he approached from the far side of the huge, curving bar. By the time she was aware of his presence, it was too late. He was already sliding lithely onto the empty stool beside her, a glass of the now-familiar bourbon-and-water in his hand.

As her head whipped around, he smiled kindly. "It won't work, Jessie." He waved his free hand in a shallow arc which took in the whole room. "I don't think there's a man out there tonight who will have the courage to try to pick you up. Not as long as your eyes are as hard and glittering as diamonds and your smile is so brilliantly cold. You're radiating pure female menace right now, honey. There's not a man in sight who will have the guts to ask you to dance."

"Except you?" she challenged too sweetly.

Lucas shook his head in response to her question, the smile edging his mouth positively lethal. "Nope, not me, either. I'm not here to ask you to dance."

Jessica's eyes narrowed as her senses registered the danger she had known lay in the depths of this man. It was as if he'd kept it hidden for the past few days. Long enough for her to convince herself that such a degree of male menace couldn't exist in civilized society.

"Really?" she dared. "Afraid I might refuse?"

"Damn right," he grinned. "I don't handle rejection well."

But he could, she thought a little wildly. He could ignore it and go after what he wanted regardless of how much rejection a woman handed out. Jessica swallowed as the realization went home. Again she tried to right her suddenly disoriented world. "If you're not going to ask me to dance, would you mind vacating that barstool? As long as you're sitting there, it's a cinch no other man will ask me to dance, regardless of my frozen smile!"

"I know. That's why I'm sitting here," he explained as if she were a child. Lucas took another sip of his bourbon and water, watching comprehension dawn on her face.

"You mean you're deliberately going to chase off anyone who might want to introduce himself?"

"Simple but effective. Consider it close surveillance."

The red stained her cheeks. "Why you arrogant...ex-cop! You know damn good and well I won't dance with you, but you've got the nerve to make it impossible for me to have any fun with someone else!"

"Where are you going?" he inquired politely as she stood up.

"As if I'd tell you!" Jessica snapped over her shoulder as she walked away from him with long sinuous strides that carried her quickly out of earshot. But not quite quickly enough.

"A ship just isn't that big, Jessie. I'll find you." The words floated after her, dark and full of promise.

And he did exactly that, over and over again as the evening progressed. He was sitting beside her as she caught the late cabaret act. He was standing in line behind her when she went through the midnight buffet. He was near enough to warn off other men when she went into the nightclubs. He never touched her, never put a hand on her. He was always just there, watching her, urging her with his eyes to accept his presence because there was no alternative for her.

It was the way it had been out in the desert, Jessica thought despairingly. He'd never put a hand on her then, either, until the fateful night when he'd led her away from the others and made love to her. By then she'd been unable to shake off his grasp and what followed had seemed inevitable at the time.

She would not allow him to turn this ship into another hunting-ground, she swore to herself again and again. It was all a matter of psychology. She had to bring herself to totally ignore his presence. It was the only way to defeat him. The difficulty lay in summoning up the willpower to ignore a man whose mere presence in a room caused her nerves to vibrate in awareness.

At one o'clock in the morning, she knew she could take no more that night. She needed sleep and a plan, neither of which she was going to get by spending her energies in useless evasion tactics. Lucas was right about one thing. The ship just wasn't big enough to get lost in for long. The only safe refuge on board was her stateroom.

Grimly she set down the last of her unfinished caviar and rose. Lucas, who was lounging across the room, watching her eat, did the same. For a moment she faced him, unaware of the other passengers who filled the room, and then she turned on her heel and left.

She thought he probably followed her, at least as far as the corridor which led to her stateroom, but she didn't see him as she stood at the door, fumbling with her key. Nevertheless, it was with a sigh of relief that she let herself inside and locked the door behind her.

Walking across to the neatly made bed, she sank wearily down onto it and tried to think, her chin in her hand. What was she going to do? Let him push her into getting off the ship in Mazatlán? Would she be able to find a flight back to the States from there without too much trouble?

The realization that she was thinking of escape startled her. She didn't need to escape, she was supposed to be safe in her own world. Oh, God. What was it he had said? When she realized that what she felt here in "reality" was the same as what she had felt out in the desert, everything would be all right.

It was all such a jumble tonight, Jessica decided sadly, slowly undoing the fastening of her black dress. She had started out feeling contrite and he had turned the tables completely. Now she was undeniably on the defensive, nervous and wary. In a matter of hours he had made her realize he had the power to make her feel the same emotions she had felt after the plane crash.

And somehow, incredible as it seemed, Jessica had the horrifying impression it had been easier for him to put her on the defensive this time, because she had learned so much more about him. Lucas Kincaid was no longer a domineering, autocratic stranger. She knew both sides of his nature, the side which could offer a woman protection or hunt her down, and the side which found satisfaction in owning a pet shop. That last made her think about his previous career.

What had it been like for him, those years in the LAPD? Jessica shuddered at the thought. A world of violence and corruption. A man would have to be a little hard to do his job effectively in such an environment. He would have to be capable of blocking off his gentler emotions in order to get on with the rough and sometimes deadly work at hand. A man who felt too compassionate or overly responsible for others would be highly subject to job burnout.

Yes, she could see why Lucas had made the decision to leave the force.

And what the hell was she doing thinking about that when she should be worrying about how to get herself out of the snare he was tightening around her? Jessica demanded of herself as she slithered out of her dress and angrily went about the business of getting ready for bed.

Knowing both sides of a man made it difficult to hate him, she realized grimly. And in some strange way, perhaps she even envied him. Lucas Kincaid had proven that he understood and could deal with the various sides of his own nature. He had accepted himself.

But when she had been forced to recognize the aspects of her own personality, which she had repressed, Jessica had fled, wanting nothing more than to turn her back on that alien, somehow threatening side of herself.

Nine

The following afternoon Jessica sought refuge in the small ship's library. It wasn't fear of Lucas that drove her into the quiet room lined with bookshelves and filled with the style of library furniture that might have been found a century ago in a stately English home. It was simply that she needed time to think and Lucas had kept her nerves on edge since breakfast. It was impossible to think clearly around him.

He had been exasperating and mildly intimidating since the moment she had arrived, a bit defiantly, at the breakfast table to find he had already ordered for her. Short of causing an embarrassing scene in front of the Howards, there wasn't anything Jessica could do except eat the food he had selected for her.

"I would have preferred the Eggs Benedict," she muttered at one point as she surveyed the plain bacon and eggs the waiter was setting before her.

"You eat whatever your man can provide." Lucas grinned unabashedly, digging into his hash browns. "Women have been doing it for years. You did it very graciously not so long ago, yourself!"

"Only because there was no alternative," she reminded him sweetly, eyes glinting as she remembered the way she had quite greedily consumed the food he had made available after the plane had gone down.

He looked up and said simply, "This morning there is no alternative for you, either. Eat."

There was a poignant pause, during which two strong wills clashed silently over the breakfast table. In the end Jessica told herself she backed down solely because she didn't wish to embarrass herself or the Howards. Picking up her fork, she smiled very brightly at the man who had somehow managed to make it seem as if he had provided breakfast. "Women may have been eating whatever their men brought home for years, but I'll bet they've been complaining about some of the selections equally long!"

"But getting fat off what was provided, nonetheless," Ann Howard broke in to advise cheerfully. "It was just a little joke, dear," she added confidingly, with a quick glance at Lucas's bland expression. "Lucas said he thought it was time you tasted some *real* food, as he called it!"

Jessica refrained from saying she wasn't in a mood for jokes at that hour of the day and smiled to show she could appreciate the humor. The smile was more than a little forced, however, because both she and Lucas knew there had been no joke involved.

The maneuver was only the beginning to a day Lucas devoted to proving his point: Incredible as it seemed, he was quite capable of duplicating on board a luxury cruise liner the same sensual tension, the same sense of hunter and hunted, the same feeling of inevitability that had assailed Jessica in the remote desert canyon several days earlier.

He was there when she went swimming, his iron-hard gaze following every movement of her body in the water as if she were an exotic species of tropical fish he planned to net. He was there with iced tea when the sun became too warm, but when she drank it, Jessica felt as if she had somehow accepted one more link in the chain he was using to bind her. Actions that in another man would have shown gentlemanly courtesy, had another meaning, coming from Lucas. There was no way to refuse most of them without appearing churlish to onlookers, but every time she accepted the smallest act of politeness, Jessica knew she was only tightening her own bonds.

There was no question of using another man as protective cover. No other man even came near her now. Even if one had been inclined to brave the glittering, nervous look in her eyes, none wanted to brave the promise of iron in the gaze of the man who was always nearby. Lucas had trapped her in a primitive, isolated little world from which escape was as impossible as it had been in the desert.

They spoke little throughout the better part of the day. Lucas seemed willing enough to talk when Jessica began a conversation, but her words generally turned scathing within a few sentences and Lucas lapsed into silence, a knowing look in his eyes. He knew how trapped she was beginning to feel, Jessica realized. Every time she came close to losing her temper, he simply waited for the explosion. Perversely, she refused to oblige him.

By the time she had resorted to seeking out the solitude of the ship's library, Jessica was very much in need of its quiet atmosphere. She sank into one of the large, wingback chairs, propping her sandaled feet on a hassock. The full skirt of her yellow-and-blue patterned sundress added a decided splash of color to the subdued room.

What was happening to her, she asked herself, staring at the rows of books on the far wall. No, she ought to rephrase that question: What was she *allowing* to happen to her? A woman had to take responsibility for her own actions and reactions and there could be no denying that her mind and her body responded with vivid awareness to Lucas Kincaid. His quiet pursuit here on the ship wouldn't have worked if she had been able to ignore his effect on her senses. At most he would have constituted an annoyance.

She should have been able to laugh at him, tell him to go to hell and mean it. But she couldn't, just as she hadn't been able to do so during those five days after the plane crash. A woman was not a mindless, helpless quarry like a rabbit. Unless he resorted to violence, a man could not force her to step into his snare, much less remain there. And if there was one thing about Lucas of which Jessica was certain, it was that he would never resort to violence.

Yet there she was, struggling in his snare. Again.

The realization made her close her eyes briefly in

dismay and confusion. When she opened them Lucas was coming through the library door, a tray in his hands.

"I didn't want you to miss afternoon tea," he drawled, placing the tray with its teapot, cups and a plate of scones beside her. "Will you pour?" he added with grave politeness as he sank easily into the chair across from her. "I believe it goes with the room."

"My pouring tea?" she murmured, glancing warily at the innocent pot.

"Umm. A feminine tradition or something."

There seemed no point in refusing and in any event she wanted a cup herself. It was only as she passed him his tea together with a scone that it struck Jessica how little the setting really mattered. She might as well have been handing him his chunk of roasted rabbit from the other side of the campfire. It felt exactly the same to her. She was serving him the food he had provided. Her hand shook a little as she acknowledged that Lucas could make the formality of afternoon tea a decidedly primitive exchange between a man and a woman.

"How did you find me?" she asked with a touch of flippancy to cover her uneasiness. Carefully she poured herself a cup of tea, using the action to avoid meeting his eyes.

"There aren't that many places on board that could afford a woman a quiet retreat." He smiled gently. "You weren't cowering in your stateroom so, by process of elimination, I tracked you here. Doing some thinking, Jessie?"

"Yes." She refused to be provoked into telling him

what she had been thinking about. Besides, he undoubtedly already knew.

He did. "Jessie, neither of us could ever ignore or escape the other," Lucas said quietly. "Are you beginning to understand that?"

"I'll admit that in an artificially confined world such as this ship it's a bit tricky," she said crisply.

"It would be the same anywhere. That's the only point I'm trying to make."

"Lucas, what do you want from me? An affair? We've already had that!"

"I told you. I want you to come and live with me. I want to give you a home where you can let the gentle side of your nature flourish. I want to be the man on whom you lavish all your softness. Don't misunderstand me; I admire your strength, a part of me likes the challenge of it and another part of me likes the idea that it can be relied upon in a thousand different ways."

"What ways?" she bit out, unwilling to admit what his words were doing to her. "You've tried to crush the strong side of me from the beginning!"

"That's not true, honey," he denied gently. "The only time I ever tried to master the strength in you was that first day after the crash and then I had no choice. I did it for your own good as well as that of the others. But I certainly didn't set out to permanently crush your spirit and you know it. A man needs strength from his woman, just as he needs softness."

"Why?" she asked starkly.

"It's the strong side of your nature that assures me I can trust you implicitly," he surprised her by saying simply. "Once you've accepted me completely with your mind as well as your body, I'll know you will never turn to another man. I'll know you'll use your power to defend our relationship, not destroy it. You see?" he concluded whimsically, "your strength is as important to me as your softness. I'm a greedy man. I want both."

Jessica swallowed, fighting down the strange rush to give him everything he wanted. It would be so easy. All she had to do was put her hand in his and let him lead her into his world. For a long moment she sat very still, staring at him and then, with a deliberate effort of will, Jessica managed to shake off the dangerous urge to surrender. But, dear lord! Each time the task of collecting her straying senses was becoming more difficult. How much longer could she continue to fight the undermining feeling of inevitability? In only a few more days they would be back in Los Angeles....

The next day in Mazatlán, Lucas arranged for Bill Howard to go out on one of the deep-sea fishing boats. The older man was overjoyed at the prospect of fishing for the big, sleek gamefish available in the Mexican waters. Jessica was, if not exactly overjoyed, definitely feeling a sense of relief as she and Ann watched the men prepare to leave on the boat they had chartered. Lucas had taken charge of renting the proper equipment and he had sought out a charter captain with whom he had worked previously. Lucas was going with Bill and therein lay the reason for Jessica's sense of relief. It was the first time she had known a sensation of freedom in days.

As if aware of her inner excitement, Lucas paused for a few minutes before joining Bill on the fishing boat. "Goodbye, Jessie. We'll be back in about four hours. In the meantime, stick with Ann like a good girl, hmmm? And both of you stay in the main tourist areas, understand?"

"Are you being patronizing, Lucas?" Jessica inquired interestedly. She wasn't certain, herself, exactly where this urge to tease him had come from.

"I'm going to be damn annoyed if you aren't waiting here on this dock in four hours," he retorted, noting the glint of laughter in her eyes. "Just remember what happened the last time you disobeyed orders, woman!"

"I do. You came gallantly to my rescue and then took me out to lunch."

He grinned, a slow, wicked promise of pure male menace. "This time it will be different."

He was teasing her, Jessica realized belatedly, precisely because he knew there was no real risk of her getting into trouble. She would stay with Ann Howard and the two of them would confine themselves to the crowded areas of town. Lucas must have had a sixth sense that told him exactly how much under his control she had slipped.

"Have fun!" Ann called out as he released Jessica to step on board the gently bobbing boat. Bill waved back at her a little absently, busy going over his rented equipment. A moment later, Lucas joined him and neither man did more than glance back once at the two women waving goodbye on the dock.

"I don't know what they think they're going to do

if they do catch anything,'' Ann grumbled good-naturedly as she and Jessica caught a cab for the shopping district along the waterfront. ''We can hardly take a marlin back on board the ship!''

Jessica laughed. ''After they get their pictures taken with the creature they'll give the fish away for local consumption, I imagine. Come on, Ann, I've heard there is some fabulous leathercraft around this part of Mexico.''

''You know, it was really very nice of Lucas to arrange this trip for Bill. I'm sure it's going to be the highlight of my husband's entire vacation, whether or not they catch any fish!'' Ann confided sometime later, ''Lucas is a very charming man, isn't he?'' They stopped to peer into a shop window.

Jessica thought about that seriously for an instant. ''He can be,'' she finally admitted cheerfully. ''He can also be incredibly annoying. Oh, look! Do you like that purse, Ann? I found one similar to it in Acapulco, but Lucas more or less talked me out of it. He said I'd probably never wear it anywhere except on vacation in Mexico!''

''Well? Isn't that a good enough reason to buy it?'' Ann countered with perfect logic.

''You're right. Why didn't I think of that?'' Without further pause, Jessica entered the small shop and made the purchase.

At lunchtime they found a restaurant serving food in a pleasant, shaded courtyard. Later they toured the main plaza, took a horse-drawn carriage tour of the town, and finally, precisely four hours later, stood waiting on the docks for the return of the fishermen.

"Oh, my goodness," Ann exclaimed as the small boat eventually came into view. "I do believe they got something!"

It was a beautiful, blue monster of a fish and judging from the ear-to-ear grin on Bill Howard's face a few moments later, it was a good bet the older man had been the successful fisherman on board. Lucas jumped lightly ashore, and helped to tie up the boat, a pleased look of satisfaction on his face.

"Did you get anything?" Jessica asked as he stepped back and the work of unloading the fish began.

"I got a lot of fun out of watching Bill land this beauty," Lucas told her lightly. And she believed him. Lucas had set out to give his companion a good day and took his pleasure in having achieved his goal. He didn't seem the least depressed about his own lack of success. A nice man. She chewed her lip at the thought. Why was it that every time she turned around there was something else about Lucas Kincaid that appealed to her? It wasn't fair!

By the time the last night on board ship arrived, Jessica was feeling more high-strung than she had ever felt before in her life. The sense of an impending climax to Lucas's pursuit was mixed now with the first hopeful glimmer of a new possibility. This was her last night trapped with him on the vessel. If she got through tonight, she would be free.

Nothing had changed in his tactics. He was still there whenever she swam or ate or read in a deck chair. He concentrated on letting her feel his power through all the little, innocuous ways a man has of making himself known to a woman. For the first time

in her life, Jessica had begun to wonder if there hadn't
always been something more than simple courtesy behind the small things men traditionally did for women.
When Lucas performed such tasks as opening a door
or ordering her food, he managed to make her totally
aware of him, totally aware that, instead of providing
her with comfort, he could just as easily have been
assaulting her, taking her.

The bizarre thought was one of many similar no-
tions that had been flickering in and out of her head
for days, Jessica realized as she dressed for their last
dinner together. Just as he had in the desert, Lucas
wanted her to acknowledge his ability to provide for
her. Perhaps now his need to force her recognition of
his strength was even stronger in some ways, because
he knew of the role that Scanlon Hotels played in her
life. His rival was not another man, whom he could
easily have defeated, but a huge, monolithic corpora-
tion.

Jessica wasn't sure what made her choose the flirty
red dress she had worn that first night, but even as she
reached for it, the gown seemed appropriate. The beginning and the ending of a trip and possibly of one
of the strangest affairs on record, she told herself with
a wry curve of her lips. Would Lucas be moving in
for the kill tonight? He had yet to pressure her back
into bed, seeming content to settle for total awareness
of his presence, instead.

But tonight was the last night they would be together. If he didn't try to consolidate his victory this
evening, he would never have another chance, Jessica
thought as she brushed her hair into its familiar sleek

knot. Tomorrow they would be in L.A. and she would be safely out of his reach again, back under the protection of Scanlon.

Of course, that was what she had told herself the last time they parted! Jessica winced at the memory, a part of her shivering with excitement at the thought of having been unable to escape him.

Damn it! What did she want? Furiously she slipped into her high-heeled shoes and headed for the door. What was the matter with her? She had been ricocheting back and forth between two extremes of emotion for several hours, until she wasn't sure she had any idea of her true feelings in the matter.

All she had to do was get through the next few hours, Jessica decided grimly as she reached for the knob of her stateroom door. By tomorrow morning everything would be back to normal. All she had to do was make it through this last night.

And then she opened the door and found Lucas waiting on the other side. Quite suddenly the possibility of surviving the night seemed remote, indeed. Jessica froze, staring up at him with all her impending surrender in her eyes.

He smiled down at her with a politeness that didn't mask the desire in his own gaze. "Ready?"

Jessica scrambled for self-control, seizing it with a force she'd never had to use before in her life. But she managed to hide that momentary betrayal of emotion, which had been in her face when she'd found him unexpectedly at her door. Deliberately she summoned her most polished smile.

"I'm ready. I believe the Howards are expecting us

for a farewell drink before we go in to dinner?"
Bravely she left the security of her stateroom and shut
the door behind her. Why did it seem as if she'd just
slammed the door of her cage—from the outside?

"They're in the lounge on the upper deck," he said,
taking her arm with a gentle firmness that sent tremors
through her.

Jessica slanted a glance up at him as they walked
along the corridor. His hair was neatly combed and
the white shirt under the corduroy jacket was crisp and
clean. She wondered idly if he'd had the cabin steward
launder it. Another tip. This trip must be costing him
a fortune, she thought guiltily. Well, it wasn't her fault
he'd followed her, she told herself in the next breath.
But perhaps he'd felt he hadn't any choice. Did she
have any choice about the final outcome of this complex, deeply sensual dance? The sense of inevitability
hung heavily about her.

They toasted the sunset with the Howards, sipping
margaritas in the cocktail lounge and enjoying the pan-
oramic view of sea and sky. The conversation was
light and easy and Bill Howard thanked Lucas once
more for the fishing trip.

"He'll be talking about it for months," his wife
chuckled.

"He deserves to talk about it," Lucas said, grinning. "It was a hell of a good catch."

"It's too bad you didn't get anything," Ann observed regretfully.

"I took great satisfaction out of having Jessie stay
out of trouble for the day," he laughed.

"Well, there wasn't much trouble to be gotten into that I could see!" Ann retorted.

"Jessie can get into trouble in the middle of nowhere," Lucas informed her. "That's why I stick so close, generally. She needs me around to keep her safe."

Jessica lifted beseeching eyes toward heaven and the others all laughed. But as they rose to go into dinner she shot him a withering glance. "I hope you're enjoying yourself, Lucas!"

"I am."

Having arrived at the table with the others, Jessica was able to make a beeline for her own menu and she had her order ready when the waiter appeared. Appalled at the small sense of triumph it gave her, she rattled off a request for raw oysters on the half shell with mignonette sauce, cucumber and dill soup, and chicken in walnut sauce. When she flashed a triumphant glance at Lucas from under her lashes, he merely laughed back at her with gleaming eyes.

The ridiculousness of her small victory brought a somewhat rueful smile to her own lips.

The last night on board. Jessica found herself wanting to enjoy it to the fullest. She felt alive and excited and rather reckless. It was a kind of high brought about by her sure and certain knowledge that Lucas wanted her and that she had only to put him off for one more night in order to be free.

At the end of dinner the Howards joined other friends, with whom they had played bridge on board, and Lucas smiled at Jessica a bit too politely. "Shall we go to the lounge?"

"So you can amuse yourself chasing off the few men who might work up the courage to ask me to dance?" she retorted.

"It passes the time," he responded calmly, taking her arm and leading her toward the door. "Besides, the band is pleasant to listen to, even if we don't dance."

"We don't dance because you haven't asked me lately!"

"I told you, I can't stand the thought of being rejected," he quipped.

They found one of the few remaining tables and ordered brandy. The band was warming up for a group of passengers determined to spend their last night on board enjoying themselves to the fullest extent. It was going to be a somewhat boisterous crowd this evening, Jessica thought, glancing around in amusement. Off to one side she saw her acquaintance from the first day, Kirk Randall, busy chatting with the redhead from the aerobics class. The woman had confided happily to Jessica that morning after class that she had been having the time of her life since she'd met Kirk. He was, it appeared, everything a woman could hope to find on a cruise ship. Jessica was forced to acknowledge privately that she, personally, hadn't missed Kirk in the least. Lucas had seen to it that there was no room in her thoughts for another man.

Couples, including the gay couple, crowded out onto the floor as soon as the music began. No one was going to waste a minute of the precious time left. Jessica sat with Lucas and watched, sipping slowly at her brandy. She wanted very much to be out there with the others and she would have given a great deal if one of the men in the room had approached her. But she knew by now that that was highly unlikely and even if one did get up the nerve, Lucas would quash the interloper in a hurry. On the other hand, she thought resentfully, he wasn't going to ask her, himself. She didn't for one moment believe his explanation about a fear of rejection. It was just another tactic, Jessica decided as she took another swallow of brandy. She wasn't sure of the purpose of this particular tactic, but Lucas never did anything without a purpose.

Under the table the toe of her sandal swung restlessly as she watched Lucas's profile. He was reclining in his chair with a catlike grace that somehow managed to stir her senses, his eyes on the dancers. What was he thinking? she wondered.

"Missing the bunnies and parakeets?" she asked, breaking the silence between them with taunting sweetness.

"They're in good hands." He shrugged. "My assistant is very reliable."

"How about Clarence? Will he rush to greet you when you walk through the door of the shop?" she persisted, unable to control her desire to provoke him tonight.

"The only time Clarence rushes anyplace is when his food is dropped into his cage. Snakes are basically lazy creatures."

"I didn't know."

He turned his head to look at her, a smile tugging at the corners of his mouth. "You'll have to come and meet him sometime."

"I'm not too fond of snakes," she said thoughtfully. She was suddenly conscious of an intense curiosity about Lucas's pet shop.

"What *are* you fond of, Jessie?" he asked quietly.

"Dancing," she returned without hesitation.

"Poor Jessie. You haven't done much of that for the past few evenings, have you?"

She shook her head, waiting for him to ask her. Surely he would tonight!

"I rather enjoy dancing, myself," he informed her in a husky, gravel-rough voice. The iron-gray eyes met hers, pinning her. "So why don't you ask me?"

Jessica blinked. "Ask you? You're supposed to ask me!" she breathed, her pulse quickening at the expression on his face. Then, before he could say anything further, she rushed on, "Lucas, will you dance with me, please?"

"Thank you," he responded politely, getting to his feet, "I'd be delighted."

Jessica allowed him to lead her out onto the floor and pull her firmly into his arms before she lifted questioning eyes to his unreadable face. "Why didn't you ask me? Why did you insist on waiting for me to ask you? And don't give me that line about rejection!"

He slid a hand along the length of her back to the base of her spine and forced her gently into the heat of his thighs. "I wanted you to realize that I'm the only man on board with whom you're free to dance," he muttered thickly, his lips in her hair.

Jessica felt the strength in his arms, knew the controlled grace of his body, and experienced a violent longing to give herself up to the power in him, if only for the course of the dance. Unable to speak for fear of revealing more than she wished, she rested her head on his shoulder and let herself be swept away on the sensual tide of the music.

Lucas made of the dance a deeply sensual, wholly compelling ritual that engaged all her senses. Heedless of the other couples on the floor, he circled her waist with both arms, leaving her no option but to entwine her hands around his neck. When her fingers found the thickness of his dark hair, he groaned almost inaudibly and used his palms to mold her intimately against him.

Jessica had no wish to fight the tightening strands of the silver snare; not just then; not while she was still relatively safe on the dance floor. The crowd around her served the same purpose as the other passengers from the plane had served as they sat grouped around the campfire. There was safety in numbers.

But if Lucas was aware of the protection she imagined around her, he didn't show it. His body seemed intent on tantalizing hers, beckoning her closer into a furnace from which there would be no escape. Deliberately he began to build the pressure, letting his fingers sear the areas of sensitive flesh bared by the red silk dress, making her aware of the hardness of his thighs, inviting her to toy with the slightly curling ends of the hair at the back of his neck.

Like a small creature tempted by the promise of pleasure just inside the trap, Jessica hesitated on the outside, willing herself to look but not touch. She was safe as long as she kept her head. She knew that much intellectually, but it didn't seem to have any influence over her emotions. Heaven help her, but tonight she wanted Lucas Kincaid.

And tonight she could not have him without surrendering.

It was that knowledge which made her lift shocked eyes to his as the music drew to a close. There in his own gaze she saw the same knowledge. She could have him but only if she gave herself completely. As his arms fell away from her, Lucas held her a moment longer with his gleaming glance.

"Go ahead, Jessie," he advised in a drawling whisper, "run one more time. I'll find you."

She stared up at him as all the conflicting emotions within her seemed to coalesce, and then she whirled and fled through the crowd of dancers, seeking a way out of the trap; searching one last time for the safety of her gilded cage.

What she found out on deck was the railing, which barred further flight even while it protected her from the depths of the sea. She came to a halt beside it, inhaling deeply of the salt-scented night air while she tried to regain her equilibrium. Her nails dug into the wood as she stared out to sea.

Why was she running? She belonged to him. Hadn't she known that from the beginning? It wasn't because he was the dominant male in the herd. Here on the ship he was only one of many men, several of whom, including the captain, surely were far more dominant in the accepted sense. It wasn't the same as it had been out in the desert, yet for her Lucas Kincaid was the only man who counted. He would always be the one man who could dominate her senses, the one man who could arouse this primitive response. He knew her in a way no other man ever would and, in turn, she knew him as thoroughly.

It was that last thought which gave her the courage to turn slowly as the tingling sense of awareness flickered to life within her. He was there in the shadows across the deck, waiting to claim her. Dark and lean and radiating a power which seemed tuned to her alone, he stood braced against the soft motion of the ship and waited.

She regarded him mutely for a timeless moment, the moonlight gleaming on her hair, the red silk whipped around her legs by the breeze.

"Jessie, I need you."

"I know," she whispered. "I know."

Wordlessly he put out his hand and Jessica stepped forward to let his fingers close around hers.

Ten

He led her down through the ship the way he had once led her out into the desert and Jessica followed willingly, drawn by the need in him and the warm lock he had on her wrist. Lucas said nothing until she turned a questioning glance up at him as they stepped from the elevator out into the corridor that led to his stateroom instead of hers.

"I don't particularly want Scanlon to be a part of this tonight," he growled softly, gray eyes caressing. "Tonight I'll provide your bed and anything else you need."

Jessica nodded, understanding, and then they were at his stateroom door. Lucas's hand shook a little as he fit the key into the lock and the sight sparked a wave of tenderness in her that made her reach out to touch his sleeve. Her aquamarine eyes were soft and gentle in the corridor light.

He glanced down at her as the door opened and Jessica thought she would melt beneath the need and the desire in his face. He was a thoroughly honest man and he deserved to know how completely she was coming to him tonight. As the door closed behind them, she moved into his waiting arms.

"I need you, Lucas. I didn't fully understand that the first time and I was too busy trying to manipulate you the second time to analyze my own feelings. But tonight I know the truth." She spoke the words wonderingly as they came alive in her mind, half-afraid to believe them yet knowing they were the right words. "I need you as much as you need me."

"I'm not sure that's possible," he confessed hoarsely, gathering her close. "But I would go out of my head if I couldn't believe there's something important in this for you, Jessie. I don't want to just take."

"You never just take," she whispered, pressing her face into the solid warmth of his shoulder. "You give and I...I guess I'm not accustomed to men who know how to give even when they're making a claim."

"Jessie!" he breathed, his hand sliding into her hair to pull it down around her shoulders. "Jessie, you are everything I need tonight and I want you so."

He buried his face in her hair as it came free at last and Jessica sighed with a longing that consumed her totally. Lucas felt the tremor go through her slender body and he forced her more closely against him, as if he would still the shiver with his own body heat. His hands tunneled under the tumbling fall of tawny

hair and then began to move achingly down her back,
burning through the red silk.

"Oh, Lucas, Lucas...I..." Her jumbled cry was
swallowed as his mouth came down on hers, making
words unnecessary. Jessica's lips parted at once for
the passionate invasion, welcoming him deep into the
honeyed secret behind her teeth.

The kiss was a preliminary uniting that restaked a
claim that could never again be denied. Lucas surged
deeply into the intimate depths, hungrily retaking what
had been his since that first time in the desert. His
tongue sought out hers, coaxing, persuading, challenging until she could do nothing but respond in kind.
The hot love-play fed their senses, invoking tremors
of mounting excitement.

Unable to resist, Jessica's gilded fingertips slid inside the opening of the corduroy jacket, probing the
strength of his shoulders. Somehow the jacket fell to
the floor in a soft heap and then she was loosening the
tie. So intent was she on finding once more the well-
remembered warmth of his bronzed skin, Jessica was
barely aware of her own red silk dress being gently
slipped to her waist.

And then a thick, muffled groan trembled in the
broad chest beneath her fingers and Lucas's hands
moved to cup her small, curving breasts. The shock of
the passionate touch stirred her deeply. He held the
soft weight of her for a moment, savoring her, and
then his thumbs began to rasp tantalizingly across the
still-shy nipples. Under his gentle, exciting insistence,
they began to bud forth eagerly, and Jessica moaned

with longing as the tips of her breasts told him of her escalating desire.

With fingers that fumbled a little under the impetus of her own passion, Jessica managed to remove the white shirt, leaving the striped tie draped around his throat, the ends hanging down his chest. She pulled away from him as the shirt fell to the floor, picking up the ends of the tie and tugging gently.

Lucas's mouth tilted in lazy passion and he let her lead him toward the single, narrow berth. At the edge she halted, still retaining her hold on the leash and smiled up at him invitingly.

"Is this what they call being led astray?" he murmured, his eyes darkening in the soft light.

"Probably. Are you worried?" she asked throatily.

"No," he admitted thickly, "I'd follow you anywhere."

"You've got that backward, Lucas. I'd follow *you* anywhere," she told him with a sudden certainty that heightened the glow of her eyes.

"Would you?" The words sounded cryptic to her ears but, before Jessica could question them, Lucas was moving his hands to her waist, sliding his palms inside the folds of the red silk dress and pushing it over her hips. It fell into a crimson froth at her feet.

Then he went down on one knee in front of her, his lips searing the silky skin of her stomach as he slowly, deliberately, began to remove the scrap of lace and satin that was all that remained of her clothing.

He drew the panties down with exquisite, teasing slowness, exploring each new inch of flesh with his mouth as it was exposed. Jessica gasped and her fin-

gers wrapped themselves deeply into the thick darkness of his hair. Her eyes closed tightly against the
rush of passion invading her bloodstream. When the
bit of lace and satin lay at her feet, she felt his teeth
in the gentlest of stinging little kisses on her thigh.
Simultaneously his hands shaped the full globes of her
buttocks, holding her still for the flick of teeth and
tongue.

"Lucas!" It was a cry and a plea and it only served
to provoke him into more of the unbearably thrilling
little kisses. His lips moved over the skin of thigh and
hip, nipping, soothing, stinging, exciting until Jessica
thought she would go mad.

Her nails slid down to his shoulders, digging into
the hard flesh as her body arched to his touch; when
she called his name again, this time in an agony of
desire, he began to climb slowly to his feet. En route,
his kisses were lavishly trailed across each breast and
then along her throat until at last he rediscovered her
mouth.

By then Jessica was trembling with the force of her
need. When he had risen to his full height in front of
her, she curved her arms around his neck and leaned
into his strength. There her body found the unmistak-
able evidence of his own rising passion and the taut,
uncompromising demand of his maleness made her
moan once again.

"Finish undressing me, Jessie," he commanded
softly. "Touch me, sweetheart. Please touch me."

She obeyed, her mouth pressed to his bare chest as
she dealt awkwardly with the buckle of his belt. Then
she found the zipper and at last he was stepping out

of the remainder of his clothing, gloriously, unself-consciously naked. Only the tie still dangled around the firm column of his throat, symbolic of the collar she had once sought to chain him with. When he removed it absently, as if only vaguely aware of its presence, Jessica smiled to herself. There was no need to chain this man. He could be trusted completely.

Jessica, pressed close against the demanding warmth of him, reveled in the power of his passion. Her fingers began to tease and toy with the curling hair of his chest, tracing it down to his waist and beyond. When her probing touch suddenly became excruciatingly intimate, Lucas growled with a fierce promise that took away her breath.

"Jessie, you've been mine since our first time together. Tonight I need to hear you admit it. Do you understand me, sweetheart?" He swung her off her feet and settled her on the narrow bed, his eyes full of the question he had just asked.

Jessica looked up at him as he towered over her in the muted light. He needed the assurance that this time she fully comprehended the extent of their relationship. "I understand, Lucas. You've been right all along. I should never have run from you. I was only running from myself."

"Jessie!"

He came down along the length of her, covering her with his heat and fierce need. She folded him close, giving way as he forced his legs urgently between her own. The roughness of his thighs was a further incitement to her spinning senses, deliciously contrasting with her softer contours. The male scent of him was a primitive fragrance she inhaled deeply. The teasing scrape of his chest hair on her aroused nipples caused her to twist sensuously against him. When she feathered his throat with her lips, Lucas rasped words of longing into her ear and his fingers stroked the skin of her shoulders as if he were stoking a delicate fire.

There in the small room Lucas concentrated on bringing all of her senses alive. This time, Jessica knew with sure, feminine instinct, there would be no doubt about the completeness of her surrender; but, by the same token there would be no doubt, either, about the totality of what he was giving in exchange. They needed each other. It was as simple and as unbelievably complex as that.

Without hesitation Lucas used his muscled weight to pin her to the bed, but the sensation was infinitely thrilling. Every time she moved, every time she arched against him or explored the length of his leg with her bare foot, he was there, enveloping her. When he raised his lower body slightly away from hers to explore the invitingly intimate area below her waist, Jessica sucked in her breath.

"Sweetheart," he breathed huskily, "I can feel the want in you. Tell me about it. Tell me of your need."

Her head shifted restlessly on the pillow, tawny hair fanning out around her. Her lashes veiled the brilliance of her sea-colored eyes. "Lucas, I would not be able to stand it tonight if you did not make love to me. I need you so desperately!" She lifted her hips against his hand, her body opening like a flower to him as he stroked the petals of her with erotic sensitivity.

"Please, Lucas! Please!" she gasped, her breath catching in her throat.

He seemed to test himself against her, letting her know the readiness of his manhood. And then he was storming her body in a rush of power that brought his name to her lips in a silent cry.

Now the captivating tenderness of his earlier lovemaking gave way to an assault on her senses. To Jessica it seemed as if he filled her, surrounded her, chained her completely, and the heady mix of sensations made it impossible to do anything else except respond. She clung to him as if he were the only reliable thing in her world and he merged them into a single, trembling entity. The shivers that coursed through one, coursed through the other, and the damp film of perspiration generated by their bodies seemed to function as a source of electrical contact binding them together.

Again and again Jessica whispered Lucas's name as she wrapped herself around his surging body, absorbing him into her very being. In turn he grated short, incredibly arousing words against the skin of her throat. As it had the night she had set out to seduce him, the gentle pitch of the ship on the sea provided a strangely exciting counter-movement to their lovemaking, as basic and elemental as the human bonding taking place on board.

The intensity of their passion spiraled quickly, forcefully out of control. There was no attempt to tease or provoke or play. Tonight the final link was being forged in a chain that would bind her, Jessica knew instinctively, to Lucas for the rest of her life. She did not question the fact, content instead to allow it to happen. Her nails raked his back in ancient meaning and when he slid a palm beneath her buttocks to raise her more tightly against him, she felt his fingers sinking deeply into her softness.

The small pain acted as a stimulant to her already overheated senses.

"Lucas!" Her words were breathless, choked as her whole body went abruptly, exquisitely taut. "I don't...I can't..."

Instead of gentling the tension in her, he muttered her name and fed it further by finding a throbbing nipple with his lip-sheathed teeth.

"Oh!" She slipped over the edge of the precipice as he thrust into her with a final flash of power. The tension that had arched her feet and throat and coiled so tightly in the pit of her stomach suddenly exploded, ricocheting back along each individual nerve ending in a series of tiny, shivering convulsions that brought indescribable pleasure to every inch of her body.

Even as she succumbed to the riveting series of sensations, Jessica was conscious of Lucas arching himself simultaneously into her, pressing her far into the depths of the bunk with his weight and strength. The reaction of his own release rippled through the muscles under her hands and Jessica gloried in the knowledge that it had been as intense as her own.

For an unknown time there was only silence in the small room. Jessica lay sprawled beneath the relaxed strength of the man who had just claimed her so completely, languidly content to stay in such a position forever. It was where she belonged. They needed each other.

When he finally lifted his tousled head to search her love-softened features, Lucas said nothing for a long moment. His clear gray eyes roved over her as if he was examining a personal treasure. Then, wordlessly he bent his head to kiss her lips in a seal of promise and commitment.

"Go to sleep, sweetheart," he whispered, rolling onto his side and pulling her close against him. "Go to sleep." He stroked her hair tenderly back from her forehead and tucked her cheek down onto his shoulder. "It's almost over."

She wanted to ask him what was almost over, but the aftermath of their passion had left her limp and drifting. She welcomed the instructions to sleep and her body obeyed without hesitation.

It was the silence of the ship around her that awakened Jessica the next morning. For a few minutes she couldn't comprehend exactly what it indicated, and then she realized they must have docked in L.A. Out in the corridor there came the sounds of people rolling suitcases along the halls, preparing to leave the ship. Opening her eyes, she glanced around and found herself still swallowed in darkness. The drawback to an inside stateroom, she thought in amusement. No window.

And then she realized that the narrow berth was empty except for herself.

"Lucas!" Anxiously she called his name into the darkness and when there was no response she fumbled hastily for the light switch. Blinking in the abrupt glare she glanced around. The small cabin had been vacated. Had Lucas already left the ship? Surely not without her!

A curious sense of panic welled up inside, driving her out of the bed and sending her scrambling for the protection of her clothes. Where was he? Why had he left? He couldn't have done this to her!

She found the note propped against the cabin door where she could not fail to find it on her way out. Nervously she reached for it and slit open the envelope, which carried the cruise liner's crest on the outside. Jessica read the short message with her heart in her throat.

Sweetheart, there is one more step which must be taken to fill the space between us and you must be the one to take it. You have to be sure, Jessie. I want you to know your own mind. I don't want an affair with you, I want to make a home with you. That means Scanlon must become merely a career and not a substitute family for you. Come to me, Jessie, when you no longer want to live in a gilded cage. I was wrong, honey, I can't reach in and force you outside. I can only open the door and ask you to come out and join me.

In the lower left-hand corner was scrawled an address. Tears burned her eyes as Jessica carefully folded the note and stuffed it into the opening of her evening bag. Then, dressed in the crimson silk she had worn the night before, she walked out into the hall and up the stairs to her own stateroom. She would have to hurry. After all, Scanlon would have a car waiting for her outside on the docks.

It was several days later that Jessica halted on the sidewalk of a pleasant, palm-lined San Diego street and glanced again at the address on the card in her hand. It couldn't be much farther, she decided with a frown of concentration as she lifted her eyes to scan the signs of the various shops and businesses along the street. Then she saw what she was looking for, a colorful wooden sign with the store's name in red letters: THE PET CONNECTION.

For the first time since she had climbed into the Scanlon car at the docks, and been driven back to her hotel apartment, Jessica's nerve faltered. What if Lucas had been trying to back out of the relationship? What if he had left the note because he thought it was a simple way for both of them to end a shipboard romance?

Then Jessica shook her head and her mouth edged upward in a smile of returning certainty. Lucas Kincaid would never have chosen to end things with a note left propped against the door the morning after. Nor would he have said anything in that note that he didn't mean. Lucas, she knew very well, was an honest man; a man who could be trusted with her life or with her love. Chin lifted, the faint smile echoed in her eyes, Jessica strode briskly toward the door of the pet shop.

She opened it and stepped inside, her arrival announced by a bell which tinkled overhead. There she halted in her tracks, eyes widening with amused interest. Pandemonium reigned.

"What the hell?" It was Lucas's voice, coming from somewhere toward the rear of the shop near a row of cages. She couldn't see him, but she could hear him quite clearly. "Whoever just came in, for God's sake shut the door!"

Jessica did so at once and then stood there trying to make sense out of the confusion. On the left a huge parrot screeched, flapping his wings as he stalked up and down his perch. He was responding to the shouts of a little boy racing down the aisle toward him, waving a net.

"I think he went this way, Mr. Kincaid!" the boy shouted happily, diving under a counter with his net. The parrot, not yet convinced the net hadn't been aimed at him, squawked again.

Several puppies could be heard, adding their excited barking to the general din, and the large cage of parakeets was a flutter of screeching activity. Green, yellow, and blue wings filled the space available as the alarmed and angry birds reacted to the clamor around them.

A cat hissed furiously as another little boy rounded an aisle full of empty goldfish bowls. This one, too, was waving a net and industriously checking under every counter as he hurried along. "He's over here, Jeff! I saw him head this way!"

A stack of tropical fish food cascaded to the floor as the other boy responded to his friend's call. Jessica watched, fascinated, as animals yelped, meowed, screeched, or raced around their cages in agitation.

The two boys were clearly enjoying themselves enormously as they threatened everything in sight with the nets.

Then something tiny and white raced across the open toe of her sandal. She looked down the length of her leg in time to see a small mouse dash for cover behind a package of dog food. Quite suddenly she knew what the nets were for.

"Over here, boys," she called cheerfully. "He went that-away."

"Where? Where?"

Mutely, Jessica pointed to the bag of dog food and the boys rushed forward. "We've got him, Mr. Kincaid!"

"Well, keep him cornered!" Lucas yelled back, starting up the aisle. "If the cats see him again there will be hell to pay!" He didn't see Jessica for a moment, his full attention on the two boys as they attempted to cage the scampering mouse with their feet while swinging the nets wildly.

Jessica took the opportunity to drink her fill of him, not bothering to hide the love in her eyes. He was wearing jeans and a white, long-sleeved shirt with the sleeves rolled up. The hard contours of his face and the lean strength of his body satisfied some of the hunger she had been feeling for the past few days. He glanced toward the door an instant later and Jessica did not try to hide the revealing expression on her face as his frowning gaze collided with hers.

"Jessie!" He came to an abrupt halt, mouse and children and general confusion clearly forgotten at the sight of her. "Jessie," he repeated in soft wonder. "You came."

"Didn't you think I would?" she returned with a tender, teasing smile.

"To tell you the truth, I was getting a little scared," he admitted starkly. "It's been several days."

"I had a lot of loose ends to tie up," she whispered.

"Jessie, I love you," he said very clearly above the general din. "I've loved you since that first day in the desert. I'll love you for the rest of my life."

"Oh, Lucas!" Aqua eyes glowing, she went toward him, throwing herself into the security of his arms with a force that was self-explanatory. "I love you, too. Why else do you think I'm here?"

"Jessie, my sweet Jessie." He held her fiercely as if he would never let her go.

"Got him, Mr. Kincaid! Here he is!"

Jessica glanced down, her cheek still pressed against Lucas's shoulder, to see one of the boys gleefully holding the hapless mouse by its tail. "Can we feed Clarence now? Can we?"

Lucas grimaced, not releasing Jessica. "You can. You know I can't bear to watch. Just be damn careful the mouse doesn't escape again, understood?"

"Yes, sir!" Together the boys raced back up the aisle toward the rear of the shop.

Jessica lifted her head to smile up at the man who held her so tightly. "Are you supposed to use language like that around children?"

"When one has been sufficiently provoked, it's unavoidable!" He gazed down at her with an urgency and a satisfaction that touched her heart. "Oh, God,

Jessie, I've missed you so. I was going to give you another week and then I would have come after you.''

"Again?" she teased lovingly, her arms resting happily around his neck.

"And again and again," he confided huskily. "Until you finally realized what you wanted."

"I want you, Lucas, and a home."

"And Scanlon?" he asked as if he had to.

"Scanlon is my company. It's a good company, Lucas. They even gave me a transfer down here to the San Diego office when I asked for it. But it's you I'll be living with. You're the only one who can give me a real home."

"Jessie, will you marry me?" he whispered.

"I was just about to ask you the same question." She grinned. "Of course, I'll marry you, Lucas Kincaid. I told you on the last night on ship that I would follow you anywhere."

"I wanted you to be sure, honey. I couldn't take it if you ever changed your mind." She saw the truth of his words in his eyes and she let her answer show in the way she pulled his head down to her own.

The two boys, returning from their snake-feeding, broke up the embrace. "It's all done, Mr. Kincaid," the taller one told Lucas helpfully, curious eyes on Jessica as she pulled herself a few inches away from Lucas. "Give Clarence about ten more minutes and there won't be any evidence left," he added proudly.

"Thank you," Lucas drawled wryly, his mouth curving in repressed amusement. "I'll see you again tomorrow. Remember to tell that new boy who moved in next door to you about Clarence."

"I sure will. Maybe his mom will see what a really terrific snake he is. My mom just didn't understand him," the boy sighed. "Come on, Jeff, let's get going. It's almost dinner time."

"Which reminds me," Lucas said softly as the shop door closed behind the two. "I've spotted the perfect restaurant for you. It's almost closing time. Give me a minute to lock up and I'll take you out to dinner."

A few minutes later, he locked the door on the now-quiet store and hooked a possessive arm around Jessica's shoulders, tugging her close against his side. "You're going to love this place, Jessie. Tailor-made for you."

"I can't wait," she chuckled, loving the proprietary feel of his arm and the warm grace of his body alongside hers. "Are you going to tell me exactly what sort of restaurant this is?"

"It's a sushi bar," he announced grandly. "Raw fish served in a thousand beautiful ways. Just your kind of place!"

She giggled. "Have you ever had sushi?"

"Nope. I've been saving the experience to share with you," he told her dryly.

"Don't worry, the Japanese have been enjoying it for years. You'll love it," she reassured him. "You know, you should be grateful I'm so fond of fish. After all, you're fond of catching them, aren't you? We make a good team."

"Precisely what I kept telling myself out there in the desert," he murmured.

"Don't give me that," she chided. "Teamwork was

not exactly what you had in mind out there and you know it!"

He started her determinedly down the sidewalk. "Jessie, that's behind us," he declared firmly, "and you know it. Don't tease me about it any more. Please!"

"Okay," she agreed easily, eyes gleaming as she slanted him a sideways glance. "Whatever you say. Boss."

"Jessie!" He swung her to a halt, rueful frustration twisting his mouth and narrowing his gaze as he glared down at her. "If you don't let the subject drop, I swear, I'll…!"

"You'll what?"

"I'll change it," he retorted very smoothly, a wicked light flaring in the depths of his eyes.

"Change it to what?" Jessica prodded in amusement.

"To the little matter of your taste for raw fish."

"What about it?" she dared.

"Have you always loved raw fish? I don't recall your pining for it in the desert."

"I've enjoyed it off and on for years, why?"

"I mean, have you always made a habit of eating it with almost every evening meal?"

"Well, no, but it was especially well prepared on the boat and tonight it sounds very good again. What are you getting at, Lucas?"

He smiled with unabashed male anticipation and then gently pulled the snare taut. "Didn't your ex-family ever talk to you about the facts of life? About the significance of certain cravings, for example?"

As his meaning dawned, Jessica's eyes went wide. She did some hasty addition and came up with some answers. "Oh, my goodness. I hadn't realized how much time…I've had so much on my mind lately and I didn't stop to think. Lucas, you don't really suppose I might be pregnant, do you?"

"You're in a better position to judge that than I am," he answered, his eyes moving over her slender figure possessively as if he hoped very much to see some early sign. Then he sobered as she continued to stare at him, lips slightly parted in bemusement. "Honey, would you mind very much if you found out you were going to have a baby?" he asked anxiously.

"I think," Jessica stated slowly, "that you would make an excellent father. I'm not so sure about my mothering capabilities. Lucas, I know very little about children."

"Don't worry, I'll start bringing home some kittens and puppies and things," he assured her happily. "You can practice on them."

"You'd like to have a baby, wouldn't you?" she marveled.

"Yes," he told her unequivocally. "I would like very much for you to have my baby. I want a family as badly as you need one, sweetheart. Don't worry, I'll be there every step of the way. I told you once I'd never abandon you under any circumstances, remember?"

"I remember." Jessica smiled, relaxing as she accepted the idea. "I guess it would be the luckiest kid on the block. His choice of almost any pet from his father's pet shop!"

"And his mother will always be able to get him into the best hotels. What kid could ask for more?" Lucas concluded, pulling her close.

"I don't know about the kid, but I can state categorically that his mother has everything she wants," Jessica murmured as his lips found hers.

* * * * *

SPECIAL EDITION

Stories of love and life, these powerful novels are tales that you can identify with— romances with "something special" added in!

Fall in love with the stories of authors such as **Nora Roberts, Diana Palmer, Ginna Gray** and many more of your special favorites—as well as wonderful new voices!

Special Edition brings you entertainment for the heart!

SILHOUETTE® *Desire®*

Do you want...

Dangerously handsome heroes

Evocative, everlasting love stories

Sizzling and tantalizing sensuality

Incredibly sexy miniseries like **MAN OF THE MONTH**

Red-hot romance

Enticing entertainment that can't be beat!

You'll find all of this, and much *more* each and every month in **SILHOUETTE DESIRE**. Don't miss these unforgettable love stories by some of romance's hottest authors. Silhouette Desire—where your fantasies will always come true....

DES-GEN

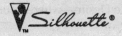

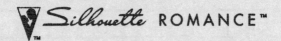

Silhouette ROMANCE™

What's a single dad to do when he needs a wife by next Thursday?

Who's a confirmed bachelor to call when he finds a baby on his doorstep?

How does a plain Jane in love with her gorgeous boss get him to notice her?

From classic love stories to romantic comedies to emotional heart tuggers, **Silhouette Romance** offers six irresistible novels every month by some of your favorite authors! Such as...beloved bestsellers **Diana Palmer, Annette Broadrick, Suzanne Carey, Elizabeth August** and **Marie Ferrarella,** to name just a few—and some sure to become favorites!

Fabulous Fathers...Bundles of Joy...Miniseries... Months of blushing brides and convenient weddings... Holiday celebrations... You'll find all this and much more in **Silhouette Romance**—always emotional, always enjoyable, always about love!

SR-GEN